THE IMITATION OF CHRIST

BOOK IV: A MEDITATION ON THE HOLY EUCHARIST

THOMAS A'KEMPIS

EPIGRAPH: A POEM BY ALFONSO S. GRECO

The Eucharist

The chemistry of this one drop
Contains the elements of all,
When sinless Master lets His Strength
On sinful servants' tongue to fall.

Within the Fibre of This Flesh,
Life's scattered proteins merge.
This Flesh is muscle for the soul,
All adipose to purge.

No mouth, however closed with sin,
Resists this virgin Bread,
Save soul and sin identified,
When mouth is closed and dead.

No food then can help them,
Swept off in damning flood.

But life of soul find higher life,
In Saviour's Flesh and Blood.

Alfonso S. Greco
March 3, 1953

CONTENTS

PART I: THE IMITATION OF CHRIST, BOOK IV

THE IMITATION OF CHRIST
BOOK FOUR
BY THOMAS A'KEMPIS

ON THE BLESSED SACRAMENT
A Devout Exhortation to Holy Communion
WITH EDITS, COMMENTS AND FICTIONAL NARRATIVE
BY TIMOTHY E. MOORE

PREFACE TO BOOK IV

I

In Book I, Thomas brought us as novices into the monastery, teaching us how to leave the world behind.

In Book II, now mature enough to handle our mission, Thomas hands us the cross we must bear, but tells us not to be afraid to carry our cross, since Jesus is helping us along the Way.

In Book III, we continue the journey. Thomas turns the magnifying glass upon our inner selves us to explore our weaknesses, directing us to the next path toward becoming Christ-like, joining Him at the Altar.

It is here, in Book IV, that we unite ourselves with Jesus through the Blessed Sacrament: The Holy Eucharist, which is the source and summit of our faith.

Thomas saves the best for last: Divine Union.

We have arrived at the altar to receive Him, and yet we must prepare in a special way. We should examine our conscience, receive reconciliation, meditate on His holy word, and empty ourselves of worldly cares or selfish curiosities.

Though this is the second shortest book, it is the most profound of the four. As with each book, revisiting chapters time and again is a worthwhile exercise, but with the fourth book, do so before approaching the Lord's Table, as a celebrant, a recipient, or as an adorer. You won't regret it.

II

The fictional narratives bring the reader to understand why and when this book was written. I put the reader into the time, place and thinking of Thomas a'Kempis in *In That Same Year, Letters from Thomas a'Kempis to Adriaan Boeyens, Three Pieces of Bread,* and *The Installation*. These works are based on much research, a personal pilgrimage to Zwolle, and prayer. I hope these bring alive the intent of Book IV.

In That Same Year, is fiction, but replicates the style and fashion of Thomas a'Kempis as he chronicles the happenings at Mt. St. Agnes. This is not the actual text, of course, but a fictionalized account. There is evidence of Thomas having a separate, personal journal, which many writers use to jot down ideas or track their thoughts. In that journal, I'm imagining what he would have had to say about this book, as he did so often in his *Chronicles of Mount St. Agnes.* Though Thomas doesn't specifically tell us, we can surmise he wrote this book last, in the late 1450's.

With the *Letters*, I'm bringing an 91 year old Thomas and twelve year old Adrian Boeyens together. Thomas firmly believed in active Discipleship. He was looking for someone to take on the mantle given him by Prior Radewyns and Thomas' brother, Jan. I wanted to then tie Thomas' holy mentorship to a youth that we know was a student of the Modern Devotion at or near Zwolle during the last years of Thomas' life. I wanted Thomas to "pass the torch" to a leader of the next generation of holy men. That youth, Adrian Boeyens, eventually was chosen by God to be Pope Adrian VI. You can read more about Adrian in Part II.

Of course, I have no direct evidence that Thomas and Adrian ever met. This is not a historical work to cite for a learned journal. Most of

Adrian's writings are lost to posterity, a strange fact since he was an academician, a prolific writer and an adviser to kings. As a reformer and a devout priest, I believe Adrian's writings were purposefully destroyed. Again, no proof. Likewise, I find his untimely death equally suspicious. As a compromise candidate for Pope, he was unpopular among the papal bureaucracy that lingered from his predecessor and were compromised by his Medici successor. In fact, Adrian was so unpopular that out of concern for his safety, he delayed coming to Rome for over seven months. That is a story for another time. However, I try to bring this to the reader's attention in the short story called *The Installation*.

Three Pieces of Bread, is a fictional narrative where Thomas' mentor, Prior Radewyns communicates by letter, to a young Thomas. Thomas holds on to the letter, even in to his old age, until he meets a young Adrian Boyens. Thomas shares the letter with Adrian as a way to persuade Adrian to become a priest. *Three Pieces of Bread* puts the reader in the dungeon with Jesus, Dismas, the Good Thief, and Gesmas, the 'Bad' Thief. In this story, I share the sacredness of the Eucharistic life our Lord carried with Him even unto death, death on a cross, and how that sacrificial death impacts both Dismas and Gesmas and the writer, a young physician named Luke. I had St. Luke as the author of the vision because the story of Dismas only appears in Chapter 23 of Luke's Gospel account.

III

The free chapter at the end of the book is the Prologue to another book I'm working on, which is called *Lord of the World*, by the late Monsignor Father Robert Hugh Benson (1871 - 1914). Like Thomas, Fr. Benson was a prolific writer. *Lord of the World* is a prescient and entertaining imagining of the modern world clash between Secular Humanism and the Church Militant. A dystopian novel, *Lord of the World* has been hailed as prophetic and relevant today though it was written in 1907.

Thank you for reading, praying and sharing the life and writings of this great saint, Thomas a'Kempis. Through his intercession, may we all imitate Christ in our daily life.

Springfield, Illinois
    June 11, 2023
    Year of the Holy Eucharist
    Feast of Corpus Christi.

1

———

SHOW GREAT REVERENCE WHEN RECEIVING CHRIST

The Voice of The Beloved

"Come to Me, all you that labor and are heavy laden, and I will give
you rest," says the Lord.
Matthew 11:28.

~

"The bread that I will give is My flesh for the life of the world."
John 6:51.

~

"Take and eat: this is My Body, which is given for you;
do this in remembrance of Me."
Matthew 26:26.

~

"Whoever eats My flesh and drinks My blood dwells in Me and I in

him....
The words that I speak to you are spirit and life."
John 6:51, 63.

Chapter Focus: Book Four opens with a paragraph on the Words of Christ.* It is significant that a book on the Eucharist opens with this meditation. Thomas then leverages this notion with several references to Scripture, comparing one holy figure to another.

Isn't it typically human to compare ourselves to others? I do it all the time. It seems we can never be worthy or measure up. Heck, by way of comparison to Thomas, I can't even spend 30 minutes in devoted prayer without some distraction. I often wonder how other people can pray that long. So I write instead.

Once Thomas opens the discussion, he brings forth the ancient archetypes as models of behavior and compares them to the reality of the human condition, moving from there to the foot of the altar with this question: How do we dare approach the God's Altar and receive Holy Communion when we don't measure up to the likes and efforts of Noah, Moses, David, Solomon, the Angels, and the Saints?

Staying positive, let's dial back our comparisons with one another instead of the Saints. Some comparisons motivate us, like the following: When it comes to receiving Holy Communion, I like to compare myself to the children who recently received their First Holy Communion; or when I witness the little old lady who struggles with her walker up the aisle to receive our Lord's Body, Blood, Soul and Divinity. I admire them and am moved to humble myself to emulate them. They are saints with a small "s".

Thomas reminds us here and throughout this chapter, of God's invitation: "Of course you don't qualify to be here, but come anyway! Come because My Son has opened the gates of Heaven for you." And then Jesus validates this promise: "Come to Me, all you that labor and are burdened, and I will refresh you." (Matt 11:28).

My recommendation is to take this book with you to Eucharistic Adoration, or read a chapter just prior to receiving Holy Communion. God will weave the power of Thomas' words with Jesus' promises by the power of the Holy Eucharist. The Lord's Table of Holy Communion will never be the same.

CHAPTER I, In Short.

1. Jesus says, "Come to Me, all you that labor and are heavy laden, and I will give you rest."

2. You command me to approach You with confidence, and to receive the food of immortality to abide with You.

3. What does Jesus mean by this most loving condescension and friendly invitation?

4. How shall I be able, in one hour, to prepare myself to receive with reverence the Maker of the world?

5. The Patriarchs endeavored to please You.

6. There is a great difference between the Ark of the Covenant with its relics, and God's most pure Body.

7. Why am I not more inflamed, considering Your holy Presence?

8. King David danced before the Ark of God with all his might commemorating the benefits bestowed on his fore-bearers.

9. While many run to various places to visit the relics of the Saints, behold, God is here present on the Altar.

10. O God, invisible Maker of the world, how wonderfully You deal with us!

11. In this Sacrament spiritual grace is conferred, lost virtue is repaired and beauty that has been disfigured by sin restored.

12. It is sad and pitiful that we are not being drawn to receiving Christ in the Eucharist.

13. If this most Holy Sacrament were only celebrated in one place in the world, people would work that much harder to attend.

SCRIPTURE MEMORY PRAYER: "Come to Me, all you that labor and are burdened, and I will refresh you." (Matthew 11:28).

Questions: How can I bring God into my body when I can hardly spend one half-hour in devotion?

Key Quote: And behold, I have You here present on the Altar, my God, the Saint of saints, the Creator of all, and the Lord of Angels.

THE TEXT OF CHAPTER 1:

Show Great Reverence When Receiving Christ.

A Devout Exhortation to Holy Communion.
The Voice of the Beloved:

"Come to Me, all you that labor and are heavy laden, and I will give
you rest," says the Lord.
(Matthew 11:28).

"...[T]he bread that I will give is
My flesh for the life of the world."
(John 6:51).

"Take, eat: this is My Body, which is given for you.
Do this in remembrance of Me."
(Matthew 26:26).

"Whoever eats My flesh and drinks My blood abides in Me and I in
him. The words that I speak to you are spirit and life."
(John 6:51, 63).

The Disciple: These are your words, O Christ, the Eternal Truth, though not all delivered at one time, nor written in one place.

Since, therefore, these are Your words, and true, all are to be received by me with thanks and with faith.

These are Your words and You have spoken them; and these words are also mine because You have delivered these for my salvation.

I willingly receive Your words from Your mouth that these may be more integrated, yes even grafted into my heart forever.

Such great and tender words! Full of sweetness and love - this encourages me.

But my sins terrify me and my unclean conscience keeps me back from approaching such great mysteries.

The sweetness of Your words invites me, but the multitude of my sins weighs me down.

2. You command me to approach You with confidence if I would abide with You, and to receive the food of immortality if I desire to obtain life and glory everlasting.

"Come," You say to me, "all you that labor and are burdened, and I will give you rest." (Matt 11:28).

Your words are oh so sweet and amiable when spoken in the ear of the sinner.

Who am I, Lord, that You should invite me as a poor and needy sinner to the Communion of Your most sacred Body!

Who am I, O Lord, that I should presume to come to You?

Behold, the Heaven of Heavens cannot contain You and yet You say "come all to Me."(1 Kgs 8:27; Matt 11:28).

3. What do You mean by this most loving condescension and friendly invitation?

How shall I dare approach You, when I am conscious of no good on which I can presume for Your favor?

How shall I introduce You into my house when I have so often provoked Your anger and displeasure?

The angels and the archangels stand with reverential awe in Your Presence. Even the Saints and the just are afraid - and still You say, "Come to Me."

Who could believe this invitation to be true, Lord, except that You said it?

And unless You commanded it who would dare to attempt to

approach Your Throne?

4. Behold Noah, a just man labored one hundred years in building the Ark, so that he, with a few others might be saved (Gen 6:9). How then shall I be able, in the space of one hour, to prepare myself to receive the Maker of the world with reverence?

Moses, Your servant, Your great and special friend, made an Ark out of incorruptible wood, which he also covered with pure gold, so that he might deposit the tablets of the Law within it. Shall I, a corrupt creature, presume so easily to receive You – the Maker of the Law and the Giver of life?

Solomon, the wisest of the kings of Israel, worked for seven years in building a magnificent Temple for the praise of Your name. And for eight days he celebrated the feast of the dedication. Solomon offered a thousand animal victims as peace offerings, and brought the Ark of the Covenant to the place prepared for it in a solemn procession, with the sound of trumpet and jubilee (1 Kings 8:6).

And I, a wretch, and the most unworthy servant, how shall I bring You into my house who can hardly spend one half-hour devoutly? What if I would spend even one half-hour as I ought!

5. O my God, how much did these Patriarchs endeavor to do to please You! Alas! What I do is so meager! I spend such short a time when I prepare myself to communicate, being seldom wholly reconciled to You, or very seldom free from all distraction!

And yet, surely in the life-giving presence of Your Divinity, no unbecoming thought should occur, nor anything created take up my mind: For it is not an angel, but the Lord of Angels that I am to entertain.

6. And yet there is a very great difference between the Ark of the Covenant with its relics, and Your most pure Body, with its unspeakable virtues. There is a difference between those sacrifices of the Law, which prefigured things to come, and the true sacrifice of Your Body, which is the fulfillment of all these ancient sacrifices.

7. Why, then, am I not more inflamed, considering Your holy Presence? Why do I not prepare myself with greater care to receive Your sacred gifts, seeing that those ancient holy patriarchs and prophets,

yes – kings and princes, with the whole people, have shown so great an affection of devotion towards Your Divine worship?

8. King David, Your devout servant danced before the Ark of God with all his might and with wild abandon commemorating the benefits bestowed in times past on his fathers (2 Sam 6:14). He made musical instruments of different kinds. He published Psalms, and appointed these to be sung with joy. He likewise often sang songs, playing upon his harp, inspired with the grace of the Holy Spirit. He taught the people of Israel to praise God with their whole heart, and to join their voices in blessing and magnifying Him every day.

If such great devotion took place then; if such remembrance took place in the praise of God before the Ark of the Covenant, how great ought to be the reverence and devotion to which I and all Christians should show in the presence of this Sacrament and in receiving the most excellent Body and Blood of Christ!

9. Many run to various places to visit the relics of the Saints, and are astonished to hear of the Saints' wonderful works; they behold the noble church buildings and kiss the Saints' sacred bones, wrapped up in silk and gold.

And behold, I have You here present on the Altar, my God, the Saint of Saints, the Creator of men, and the Lord of Angels.

Often in seeing these things people are moved with curiosity - the novelty of the sight but experience little fruit of amendment - especially when people lightly run here and there, without any true contrition for their sins.

But here, in the Sacrament of the Altar, You are wholly present, my God, the Man Christ Jesus. Here is reaped the plentiful fruit of eternal salvation, as often as You are worthily and devoutly received.

And to this we are not drawn by any levity, curiosity, or sensuality but by a firm faith, a devout hope, and a sincere charity.

10. O God, the invisible Maker of the world, how wonderfully You deal with us! How sweetly and graciously You order all things in favor of Your elect, to whom You offer Yourself to be received in this Sacrament!

For this exceeds all of our understanding. This in a particular manner engages the hearts of the devout, and enkindles their love.

For Your true faithful followers, who dispose their whole life to amendment by this most worthy Sacrament, frequently receive a great grace of devotion and love of virtue.

11. Oh, the wonderful and hidden grace of this Sacrament, which only the faithful of Christ know, but unbelievers and such as are in bondage to sin cannot experience. In this Sacrament spiritual grace is conferred, lost virtue is repaired in the soul, and beauty disfigured by sin returns again. And so great sometimes is this grace that from the abundance of devotion that is bestowed, that not only the mind, but the frail body also feels a great increase of strength.

12. It is sad and pitiful that we are so lukewarm and negligent to the point of not being drawn to the receiving of Christ. In Jesus consists all the hope and merit of those that shall be saved, for He is our sanctification and our redemption. He is our comfort in our pilgrimage and the eternal beatitude of the Saints. Therefore, it is much to be lamented that many regard this saving mystery so lightly in which Heaven rejoices and the whole world is preserved. Oh, the blindness and hardness of your heart! Such an unspeakable gift, not highly prized from daily use, quickly falls into its disregard.

13. For if this most Holy Sacrament were only celebrated in one place and consecrated by only one priest in the world, wouldn't you have a great a desire to go to that place and to such a priest of God, so that you might see such divine mysteries celebrated? But thankfully, now there are made many priests, and Christ is offered up in many places, that the grace and love of God to all mankind may appear the greater, the more this Sacred Communion is spread throughout the world.

Thanks be to You, O Good Jesus, our Eternal Shepherd, Who has promised to feed us poor exiles with Your precious Body and Blood, and Who invited us to receive these mysteries with the very words of Your own Mouth, saying: "Come to Me, all you that labor and are burdened, and I will refresh you." (Matt 11:28).

*"In the beginning was the Word...."(John 1:1).

2

———————

GOD'S GREATNESS AND CHARITY ARE SHOWN TO ALL IN THE SACRAMENT

Chapter Focus: From "Back to the Future" to "Star Trek" to "Avengers Endgame," we are fascinated by time travel which seems to be the stuff of science fiction and fantasy. But not to us. And not to God. For example, when I drive by the neighborhood where I grew up, I pray backward in time. When I visit the Church of my childhood, I pray God's blessing upon all the servants of God: Monsignors Day and Dirksen; Fathers O'Shea and Porter; Sisters Mary Gloria, Luke, Dominic and others. They taught me about the Sacraments and brought me to the Altar of Holy Communion. Of course, I learned at home, too, but in this Chapter, Thomas addresses the Priests and Religious, so I will too. We can't travel in time without our navigators and time keepers.

We witness time travel at every Mass when, at the Consecration of Bread and Wine at Holy Mass, the priest elevates the Host. By participating and receiving Holy Communion, we truly receive the Lord Himself - we are there in the Upper Room, at the Last Supper, time traveling - back to Holy Thursday, Good Friday, Holy Saturday and Easter Sunday. Christ's sacrifice is timeless, His love undiminished, His offering of Himself inexhaustible and unquenchable like the burning bush (Ex 3:2-3). God is the ever-present "I AM."

Otherwise paralyzed in our sin, we only draw near because He invites us (Jn 2:39). He is All-Holy. And because of His holiness we instantly recognize that we are unworthy to receive the gift of Himself. To fix this contradiction, He pours out His grace upon us to cleanse us from all unrighteousness (1 Jn 1:9). In holy humility and condescension, He humbles Himself by presenting His Flesh as Bread and His Blood as Wine. But He is fully there, Body, Blood, Soul and Divinity under those accidents* of reality.

Our Lord Jesus Christ asks us to receive Him over and over again, thereby showing His bounteous generosity as well as reminding us to remember His sacrifice until He comes again (1 Cor 11:26).

Come, Lord Jesus, Maranatha!

CHAPTER 2, In Short.

1. Trusting in God's goodness and great mercy, draw near to the Fountain of Life.

2. Reverence and thanksgiving are due to You, Jesus, for receiving Your sacred Body and Blood.

3. Christ is the Saint of saints, and I am the lowest of sinners.

4. From where does love proceed?

5. God gives Himself to us in bread and wine and becomes our inexhaustible food.

6. Rejoice, O my soul, and give thanks to God for so great a gift.

SCRIPTURE MEMORY PRAYER: "Christ Jesus came into the world to save sinners: Of these, I am the foremost."(1 Timothy 1:15).

Question: Have you let the King feed you?

Key Quote: The charity of Christ never grows less, and the greatness of His sacrifice is never exhausted.

THE TEXT OF CHAPTER 2:

God's Greatness and Charity Are Shown To All in the Sacrament.

The Disciple: Trusting in Your goodness and great mercy, O Lord, I draw near, the sick to the Healer, the hungering and thirsting to the Fountain of Life, the poverty-stricken to the King of Heaven, the servant to the Lord, the creature to the Creator, the desolate to my own gentle Comforter.

But who am I that You should come to me (Lk 2:43)? Who am I that You should offer me Yourself? How does a sinner dare to appear before You? And how can You promise to come to me, the sinner? You know Your servant, and You know that nothing good is within me for which You should grant this grace. I, therefore, confess my own vileness while I acknowledge Your goodness. I praise Your tenderness and I give You thanks for Your great exceeding love. You do this for Your Own sake and not because of my merits so that Your goodness may be more apparent to me, Your charity more abundantly poured out upon me, and Your humility more perfectly commended to me. Therefore, because this pleases You and You have commanded it to be so, Your condescension pleases me also: oh I pray that my iniquity may not hinder it.

2. O most sweet and tender Jesus, what reverence, what giving of thanks is due to You with perpetual praise for the receiving of Your sacred Body and Blood, the dignity of which no one has been found able to express it. But what shall I think about during this Communion when approaching my Lord, Whom I am not worthy to honor and nevertheless Whom I long to devoutly receive? What could be a better and more healthful meditation for me than the utter humbling of myself before You, and exaltation of Your infinite goodness towards me? I praise You, O my God, and exalt You forever. I have no regard for myself and cast myself down before You into the deep of my sinfulness.

3. Behold, You are the Saint of saints and I the greatest of sinners (1 Tim 1:15). Behold, You stoop down to me who am not worthy to look

upon You. Behold, You come to me: You desire to be with me and You invite me to Your feast. You want to give me the heavenly food and bread of angels to eat; none other, in truth, than Yourself, the living Bread which comes down from Heaven and gives life to the world (Jn 6:51).

4. Behold, from where does this love proceed! what manner of condescension shines forth here? What great thanksgiving and praise are due to You for these benefits! Oh, how salutary and profitable is Your purpose when You ordained this sacrament! How sweet and pleasant is the feast when You gave Yourself for food! Oh, how admirable is Your working, O Lord, how mighty Your power, how unspeakable Your truth! For You spoke the Word and all things were made and done just as You have commanded (Gn 1:3).

5. It is a wonderful thing and worthy of faith and surpassing all the understanding of all that You, O Lord my God, very God and very Man, give Yourself altogether to us under a small form of bread and wine and without being consumed, You become the inexhaustible food of the receiver (Ex 3:2-3). You, O Lord of all, Who have need of nothing, have deigned to dwell in us through Your Sacrament.

Preserve my heart and my body as undefiled so that with a joyful and pure conscience I may often be able to **[celebrate, and] receive to my perpetual health Your mysteries: which You have consecrated and instituted both for Your own honor and for a perpetual memorial.

6. Rejoice, O my soul, and give thanks to God for so great a gift and precious consolation left to us in this vale of tears. For as often as you call this mystery to mind and receive the Body of Christ, you likewise celebrate the work of your redemption and are made partaker of all the merits of Christ. **For the charity of Christ never grows less, and the greatness of His sacrifice is never exhausted.**

Therefore, by continual renewal of your spirit, you ought to dispose yourself here and weigh the great mystery of salvation with attentive consideration. So great, so new, and so joyful ought it to appear to you that when you come to Communion, let it be as if for the first time, as if Christ were descending into the Virgin's womb and becoming Man this day, or as if today He were hanging on the Cross, suffering and dying for the salvation of us all.

```
                    *accidents.

    **The words in brackets pertain to a Priest
                celebrating Mass.
```

3

___

IT IS PROFITABLE TO COMMUNICATE OFTEN

Chapter Focus: My parents walked me down the aisle of St. Anne's Church. Friends and family gathered about. They left me at the altar to receive my bride, Donna. I waited in anticipation when the chords sounded the opening of the vestry doors, revealing Donna in all her beauty (Yes, Bob, Donna's father, was there too!).

Jesus waits for us in that way. And we wait for Him. We walk down the aisle and receive Him, and He receives us. Likewise, as Disciples we approach the altar to receive Holy Communion, overwhelmed by God's goodness, grace, and generosity.

As Disciples, we pine for frequent Communion as a means to sustain us on our daily walk through life, where we become weak with temptation and laziness. Like the Hobbits of the Shire, we need our Lambas Bread to feed us throughout the journey. Holy Communion helps us "draw back from evil and strengthen us for good."

Thomas suggests a principal to follow: Like a bridegroom thinks of his bride, keep God continually on your mind in order to receive Him with a devout spirit. When we grasp the significance of receiving Him in the Eucharist, our one response should be joy.

Say "Amen." Say "I do."

CHAPTER 3, In Short.

1. I come to You, O Lord, that I may be blessed through Your gift.

2. Give me Yourself, it is enough.

3. From our youth the imaginations of our hearts are evil.

4. Our Lord condescends to come to us to appease our hunger even though we are poor and weak.

SCRIPTURE MEMORY PRAYER: "Gladden the soul of Your servant; to You, O Lord, I lift up my soul." (Psalm 86:4).

Question: Can you make the effort to receive Holy Communion at least one additional time this week? What would it take to do this?

Key Quote: Without You I cannot be, and without Your visitation I have no power to live.

THE TEXT OF CHAPTER 3:

It Is Profitable To Communicate Often.

The Disciple: Behold I come to You, O Lord, that I may be blessed through Your gift. Make me joyful in the holy feast which You, O God, in Your goodness have prepared for the poor (Ps 68:11). Behold, in You is all that I can and ought to desire, You are my salvation and redemption, my hope and strength, my honor and my glory. Therefore rejoice in the soul of Your servant today, for to You, Lord Jesus, I lift up my soul (Ps 86:4). I long to receive You devoutly and reverently. I desire to bring You into my house, so that with Zacchaeus I may be counted worthy to be blessed by You and numbered among the children of Abraham (Lk 19:9). My soul has an earnest desire for Your Body and my heart longs to be united with You.

2. Give me Yourself and it is enough, for besides You no comfort provides relief. **Without You I cannot be, and without Your visitation I have no power to live.** And therefore I must draw close to You often, and receive You for the healing of my soul, lest by chance I might faint along the way if I am deprived of such heavenly food. For You once said, most merciful Jesus, preaching to the people and healing many sick, "I will not send them away hungry to their homes, for fear that they may faint along the way (Matt 15:32)." Therefore, deal with me now in like manner, for You left Yourself for the consolation of the faithful in the Blessed Sacrament. For You are the sweet refreshment of the soul.

Whoever eats worthily shall be a partaker and inheritor of eternal glory. Because I often slide backwards and sin, and quickly become cold and fainthearted, it is important for me to renew myself: I cleanse and enkindle myself by frequent prayers and penitences through receiving of Your sacred Body and Blood. Otherwise, by waiting too long I might easily fall short of my holy resolutions.

3. From our youth the imaginations of our hearts are evil, and unless divine medicine helps us, we slide away and continually grow worse (Gn 8:21). Holy Communion draws us back from evil and strengthens us for good. For if I am now so negligent and lukewarm when I communicate [or celebrate*], how should it be with me, if I do not receive this medicine, and do not seek so great a help? [And though I am not fit every day nor well prepared to celebrate Mass, I will nevertheless give diligent attention in time, in order to receive the divine mysteries, and to become partaker of so great a grace*]. For this is the one principal consolation of a faithful soul: so long as it is absent from You in mortal body, that being continually mindful of its God, it receives its Beloved with a devout spirit.

4. Oh what a wonderful condescension of Your pity surrounds us, that You, O Lord God, Creator and Quickener of all spirits, should see fit to come to such a poor, weak soul, and to appease its hunger with Your whole Divinity and Humanity. Oh happy mind and blessed soul,

to which the gift is granted devoutly to receive You its Lord God and in so receiving You to be filled with all spiritual joy! Oh how great a Lord it entertains, how beloved a Guest it brings in, how delightful a Companion it receives, how faithful a Friend it welcomes, how beautiful and exalted a Spouse, above every other Beloved it embraces, One to be loved above all things that can be desired! Oh my most sweet Beloved, let Heaven and earth and all the glory of them be silent in Your presence. Whatever praise and beauty they have it is of Your gracious bounty and they shall never reach the loveliness of Your Name, Whose Wisdom is infinite (Ps 147:5).

```
*The words in brackets pertain to a Priest
        celebrating Mass.
```

4

MANY GOOD GIFTS ARE BESTOWED ON THOSE WHO COMMUNICATE DEVOUTLY

Chapter Focus: As a little boy, as we shined our shoes on Saturday night in preparation for Sunday Mass, I remember asking my Dad, Jim, why we go to Holy Communion. "Because it strengthens us," he said. Now at that time, I believed my father to be the strongest man alive. He was an electrician. He built our house - seemingly by himself (although the neighbors helped a little!). And he loved each of us 11 children. I never saw him worry or fear anything. Looking back, I still see his rough hands and taught arms wrestling with wires or turning a post hole digger. He'd look up, wipe the sweat from his brow, point to his bicep and say, "someday you'll do this just as easily."

I say all that because in my boyhood mind I thought Dad's super-strength came from receiving Holy Communion. Really. I imagined the day when I'd receive, and thought how strong I'd become. Strong like Dad. Well, it happened, but not in the way of fulfilling the fantasies of a boy.

There are many gifts inherent in receiving Holy Communion. We can each grow stronger, like Dad, by our realization of Christ's True Presence in the Eucharist. Or by recognizing God's humility in letting us receive Him in the forms of bread and wine, to be digested into our very bodily make-up. A third way is to know that while we are receiving Christ, we are also receiving forgiveness and remission of sins.

But we have to prepare ourselves to receive Him in body, mind and spirit. Like shining our shoes the night before, we should shine up our body by fasting at least one hour before receiving Holy Communion. Back in Dad's day, you couldn't eat anything on Sunday until you went to Church. More on such preparation in Chapters 6 and 7.

We should prepare our minds by accepting the great mystery before us, and being teachable to the theology behind the True Presence. Read the Scriptures on the Last Supper as told by Saints Matthew, Mark and Luke (Matt 26, Mark 14, Lk 22). Or read the Bread of Life discourse in Chapter 6 of Saint John's Gospel. I am not saying the mystery will be solved, but rather that knowing the Scripture will help you prepare to receive this great gift.

As we near the climax of the Mass, as we call out "Lamb of God, Who takes away the sins of the world, have mercy on us!" we reach the heart of our preparation for receiving Holy Communion. We then repeat the words of the Centurion: "Lord, I am not worthy that You should enter under my roof, but only say the Word and my soul shall be healed (Matt 8:8)." At this request, our Lord always says "Yes" to us. He wants us to have the gifts of grace, of Himself, hidden under the species of bread and wine. We can never be fully worthy to receive Him, but we can have a penitent heart by creating a clean house before receiving Him. We answer Him like the Centurion: With our "Amen" we acknowledge our belief in Christ's words that His Bread is True Food and His Blood True Drink.*

We should prepare our spirit by humbling ourselves; prayerfully receiving the Host and offering that prayer back to God for our intentions. For example, today I offered my Communion for the repose of the soul of my Dad.

Now, go shine your shoes!

∾

CHAPTER 4, In Short.

1. Enable me to draw near to Your glorious Sacrament.

2. I draw close to You with hope and reverence, and truly believe that You are here present in the Sacrament.

3. In the Blessed Sacrament You have bestowed many good things on Your elect.

4. You, Jesus, will supply whatever is lacking within me.

5. Lord, grant that by coming to Your mysteries that my devotional zeal may increase.

~

SCRIPTURE MEMORY PRAYER: "Taste and see that the Lord is good; blessed is the stalwart one who takes refuge in Him." (Psalm 34:9).

Question: What gifts has God given to you when you receive Holy Communion?

Key Quote: Illuminate, also, my eyes to behold this great mystery, and strengthen me that I may believe it with undying faith.

~

THE TEXT OF CHAPTER 4:

Many Good Gifts Are Bestowed Upon Those Who Communicate Devoutly.

The Disciple: O Lord my God, present Your servant with the blessings of Your sweetness, so that I may be enabled to draw near worthily and devoutly to Your glorious Sacrament. Awaken my heart towards You, and deliver me from heavy slumber. Visit me with Your salvation that in spirit I may taste Your sweetness, which plentifully lies hidden in this Sacrament as in a fountain (Ps 34:9).

Illuminate, also, my eyes to behold this great mystery, and strengthen me that I may believe it with undying faith. For it is Your word, not human power. It is Your holy institution, not a human invention. For no one is found fit to receive and to understand these things, which transcend even the wisdom of the Angels. What portion then shall I, an unworthy sinner, who am but dust and ashes, be able to search into and comprehend of so deep a Sacrament?

2. O Lord, in the simplicity of my heart, in good and firm faith, and according to Your will, I draw close to You with hope and reverence, and truly believe that You are here present in the Sacrament as both God and Man. Therefore, it is Your will that I receive You and unite myself to You in charity. For that reason I plead for Your mercy, and implore You to give me Your special grace, so that I may be wholly dissolved in You and overflow with Your love, and no more concern myself with any other kind of consolation. For this most high and worthy Sacrament is the health of the soul and the body, the medicine of all spiritual sickness. Here I am healed of my sins and my passions are bridled. My temptations are conquered or weakened and more grace is poured into me. My virtues which have began anew are increased, my faith made firm, hope strengthened, and charity enkindled and enlarged.

3. For in this Sacrament You have bestowed many good things and still bestow them continually on Your elect who communicate devoutly, O my God, Lifter up of my soul, You are the repairer of human infirmity, and giver of all inward consolation. For You pour into us consolation against all sorts of tribulation, and out of the deep of our own misery You lift us up to the hope of Your protection, and with every new grace, You inwardly refresh and enlighten us; so that we who feel anxious and without affection before Communion, are afterwards being refreshed with heavenly food and drink. We find ourselves changed for the better. And even in such ways when You deal severally with Your elect, You do so to allow us to truly acknowledge and clearly make proof that we have nothing whatsoever of our own, and what goodness and grace come to us from You; because we ourselves are cold, hard of heart, and profane, but through You we become fervent, zealous, and devout. For who is coming humbly to the fountain of sweetness that does not carry away from there at the least some bit of that sweetness? Or who when standing by a large

fire, does not feel a little of its heat (Heb 12:29)? You are perpetually full and overflowing fountain, a fire continually burning, and never going out (Ex 3:2-3).

4. If I am not allowed to draw from the fullness of the fountain, nor to drink until satisfied, I will still work to set my lips to the mouth of the heavenly pipe, that at least I may receive a small drop to quench my thirst, that I dry not up within my heart (Jn 4:13-14). And if I am not yet able to be altogether heavenly and so enkindled as the Cherubim and Seraphim, I will still work to enter into devotion, and to prepare my heart, so that I may gain from it, even if it is only a small flame of the divine fire, through the humble receiving of the life-giving Sacrament. But whatever is lacking within me, O merciful Jesus, Most Holy Saviour, You will supply out of Your kindness and grace; You Who have promised to call all to You, saying, "Come to me, all you that are weary and heavy laden, and I will refresh you (Matt 11:28)."

5. Indeed, I labor in the sweat of my face, I am tormented with sorrow of heart, I am burdened with sins, I am disquieted with temptations, I am entangled and oppressed with many passions, and there is none to help me, there is none to deliver and ease me; none but You, O Lord God, my Saviour, to whom I commit myself and all things that are mine, so that You may preserve me and lead me to life eternal.

Receive me to the praise and glory of Your Name, You Who have prepared Your Body and Blood to be my meat and drink. Grant, O Lord God my Saviour, that with coming often to Your mysteries the zeal of my devotion may increase.

*N.b. One more observation: Thomas quotes Matt 11:28 in paragraph 4: "Come to Me, all you that are weary and heavy laden, and I will refresh you." Thomas uses the quote, as in Ch 1, to remind us that Christ calls us to Communion with Him, even though we are unworthy. While the quote is not from the Last Supper, it hearkens to the deep wisdom of accepting the challenge of His teaching.

5

ON THE DIGNITY OF THE SACRAMENT AND THE OFFICE OF THE PRIEST

Chapter Focus: I have been blessed by many good, holy priests, as well as other wonderful Christian leaders. Most, if not all, have followed the precepts Thomas lays out below. An intentional striving toward holiness is taken on by these men and women. They work to imitate Christ in self-sacrifice. They cultivate holiness by their prayers and deeds. The Pastor's life is not an easy life, especially in the modern world.

Thomas speaks from the heart, from his own experience as a priest among clergy who were often chided for their laxity and worldly natures. The Modern Devotion sought to reset the holiness bar and inculcate levels of trust with God's people: trust was in short supply following the ravages of the Plague and the shake up of the feudal hierarchy. This return to simplicity, reverence and following *The Way* of our Lord resulted in an expansive growth of devout followers to the practices of the Modern Devotion. An increase in vocations to the priesthood and religious life followed. The time for imitation piety was over. The time of imitation of Christ had arrived.

This is still a challenge today: beyond everything else, what we desire from our priests and our faith leaders is a Godliness in word and deed. Of course, you can be an excellent theologian, homilist, and preacher; as well as gregarious and friendly - evidencing joy. But if you are a Priest of God - a Good Shepherd, your striving for holiness and your transparency in pursuit of that holiness as the leader of a congregation must out-shine everything else. While I recall each priest that has passed through my life, I recall best those who were holy. For my dear Christian friends who are not Catholic, the same applies to your Pastors and congregational leaders. One of my favorite Pastors (you know who you are) is a poster-child for joy. My sister, Marie, is a tremendous example of Godliness and faithfulness. There are many others.

To all the Priests in my life (past, present and future): Thank You!

To all the Christian leaders in my life: Thank You!*

~

CHAPTER 5, In Short.

1. Even if You had angelic purity and the holiness of John the Baptist, you would not be worthy to receive or to minister this Sacrament.

2. You must believe that God Almighty is in this Sacrament.

3. A priest takes Christ's place to pray to God for himself and for the people: always remembering the Passion of Christ.

~

SCRIPTURE MEMORY PRAYER: "[O]ur citizenship is in Heaven, and from it we also await a Savior, the Lord Jesus Christ." (Philippians 3:20).

Question: Are you praying for your Priests, Deacons, and Ministers?

Key Quote: God is the principal Author and invisible Worker, to Whom all that He wills is subject, and all He commands are obedient.

~

THE TEXT OF CHAPTER 5:

On the Dignity of the Sacrament
and the Office of the Priest.

The Voice of the Beloved: Even if You had angelic purity and the holiness of holy John the Baptist, you would not be worthy to receive or to minister this Sacrament. For this is not deserved by the merit of men that a man should consecrate and minister the Sacrament of Christ, and take for food the bread of Angels (Ps 78:25). Vast is the mystery, and great is the dignity of the priests, to whom is given what is not granted to Angels. For priests only, rightly ordained in the Church, have the power of consecrating and celebrating the Body of Christ. The priest indeed is the minister of God, using the Word of God by God's command and institution. Nevertheless **God is the principal Author and invisible Worker, to Whom all that He wills is subject, and all He commands are obedient.**

2. Therefore, you must believe God Almighty is in this most excellent Sacrament, more than your own sense or any visible sign at all. Therefore, approach this work with fear and reverence.

Take heed therefore and see what ministry is committed to you by the laying on of the Bishop's hands (1 Tim 4:16). Behold, you are made a priest and are consecrated to celebrate Holy Mass. See now that you do it before God faithfully and devoutly at due time, and show Yourself blameless. You have not lightened your burden, but are now bound with a strict bond of discipline, and are pledged to a higher degree of holiness.

A priest ought to be adorned with all virtues and to set an example of good life for others (Titus 2:7). His conversation must not be with the popular and common ways of people, but with Angels in Heaven or with perfect Disciples on earth (Phil 3:20).

3. A priest clad in sacred garments takes Christ's place so that he may pray to God with all supplication and humility for himself and for the whole people. A priest must always remember the Passion of Christ: Before him he bears the cross on the chasuble*, that he may

diligently behold the footsteps of Christ and fervently work to follow after them. Behind him he is marked with the cross, that he may mildly suffer for God's sake no matter what adversities befall him from others. He wears the cross before, that he may bewail his own sins; and behind, that through compassion, he may lament the sins of others, and know that he is placed in the midst, between God and the sinner. He should not grow weary of prayer and the holy Oblation, until he deserves to obtain grace and mercy.

When the priest celebrates Holy Mass, he honors God, gives joy to the Angels, builds up the Church, helps the living, has communion with the departed, and makes himself a partaker of all good things.

*CHASUBLE: an outer garment worn by a priest during the celebration of Mass.

6

A PETITION CONCERNING PROPER PREPARATION FOR COMMUNION

Chapter Focus: A short, prayerful reflection from Thomas to set the tone for receiving Holy Communion. Thomas helps us recognize our unworthy nature as compared to God's greatness. He composes an earnest prayer, pleading for a spiritual exercise to better the soul for receiving Holy Communion. That prayer is answered in Chapter 7: Examination of Conscience. Read on. Pray on.

~

Chapter 6, In Short.

1. When approaching Holy Communion, my spirit is confused by my unworthy nature.

2. Teach me to prepare my heart for You, so that I may receive Your Sacrament.

~

SCRIPTURE MEMORY PRAYER: "Therefore whoever eats the bread or drinks the cup of the Lord unworthily will have to answer for the Body and Blood of the Lord." (1 Corinthians 11:27).

Question: How do you balance your unworthy nature against God's promise of Mercy?

Key Key Quote: [I]t is worth-while to know how I ought to prepare my heart devoutly and reverently for You.

~

THE TEXT OF CHAPTER 6:

A Petition Concerning Proper Preparation for Communion.

The Disciple: When I consider Your greatness, O Lord, and my own unworthy nature, I tremble to excess, and am confused within my spirit.

For if I do not come to You in Holy Communion, I fly from life; and if I intrude myself into the Sacrament while unworthy, I run into Your displeasure.

What then shall I do, O my God, my helper and my counselor in necessities?

2. Please, Lord, teach me the right way. Lord, please propose some short exercise suitable for receiving Holy Communion. **For it is worth-while to know how I ought to prepare my heart devoutly and reverently for You,** with full intention that I may receive Your Sacrament to my soul's betterment, or for celebrating so great and divine mystery.

THE EXAMINATION OF CONSCIENCE AND RESOLUTION OF AMENDMENT

Chapter Focus: Chapters 6 and 7 should be read together. Chapter 6 leads naturally into 7, since in Ch. 6, Thomas just asked our Lord for clarity and humility and guidance on preparing to receive Holy Communion. Thomas readily admits that he is unworthy to receive the Blessed Sacrament, or to celebrate its mysteries. And yet he is compelled and commanded by our Lord Jesus Christ to receive. Thomas pleads for our Lord to teach him the right way - with suitable exercises to prepare his soul for devout reception.

And the Voice of Christ does not disappoint.

In Chapter 7, the "so" chapter, Jesus directs the Priest and Disciple to exercise full humility, full faith, full contrition; heart, mind and soul, into the celebration and reception of the Holy Eucharist. God wants us to be free of the shackles of sin to approach the throne with boldness (Heb 4:16).

The Voice of Christ then provides a reflection that caused me great unease in recognizing my own unworthiness in receiving so great a gift from God. There are 19 lines of "so", each with a comparison of some worldly craving balanced against some related spiritual discipline. I tried to pick a favorite, best bad choice, but decided they all applied. A cop-out, I know. Frankly, I think Thomas lets us off easy as I can think of many other "So's" that are equally convicting. Perhaps this is a good opportunity to post this list on my nightstand or on the refrigerator.

This is what the Voice recommends.

We are to offer ourselves to Christ on the altar of the heart as a perpetual whole burnt-offering. We must truly repent, and draw near to Him as a result.

So easily said, so difficult to accomplish.

CHAPTER 7, In Short.

1. The priest of God must draw near, with all humility of heart with full faith, to celebrate, minister, and receive this Sacrament.

2. Sigh and grieve and be sorry, because of our carnal and worldly nature.

3. When you have confessed your shortcomings, make a firm resolution to amend your life.

SCRIPTURE MEMORY PRAYER: "None of the crimes [you have] committed shall be remembered against [you; you] shall live because of the justice [God] has shown." (Ezekiel 18:22.)

Question: Which of the "So's" cause you the greatest discomfort?

Key Quote: For there is no oblation worthier, no satisfaction greater for the destroying of sin, than that you offer yourself to God purely and entirely with the oblation of the Body and Blood of Christ in Holy Communion.

THE TEXT OF CHAPTER 7:

The Examination of Conscience
and Resolution of Amendment.

The Voice of the Beloved: Above all things the Priest of God must draw near with all humility of heart and supplicating reverence, with full faith and pious desire for the honor of God to celebrate, minister, and receive this Sacrament.

Diligently examine your conscience and with all your might, with true contrition and humble confession cleanse and purify it, so that you may feel no burden, nor know anything which brings you remorse and impedes approaching freely.

In general, have displeasure against all your sins and especially be sorrowful and mournful because of your daily transgressions. If you have time, confess to God all miseries of your passion within the secret of your heart.

2. Sigh and grieve and be sorry, because you are still so carnal and so worldly:

so unmortified from your passions, so full of the motion of concupiscence;

so unguarded in your outward senses, so often entangled in many vain fancies;

so much inclined to outward things, so negligent of internal;

so ready to laughter and ill-discipline, so unready to weeping and contrition;

so prone to ease and indulgence of the flesh, so dull to zeal and fervor;

so curious to hear novelties and behold beauties, so unwilling to embrace things humble and despised;

so desirous to have many things, so grudging in giving, so close in keeping;

so inconsiderate in speaking, so reluctant to keep silence;

so disorderly in manners, so inconsiderate in actions;

so eager after food, so deaf towards the Word of God;

so eager after rest, so slow to labor;

so watchful after tales, so sleepy towards holy watchings;

so eager for the end of them, so wandering in attention to them;

so negligent in observing the hours of prayer, so lukewarm in celebrating, so unfruitful in communicating;

so quickly distracted, so seldom quite collected with yourself;

so quickly moved to anger, so ready for displeasure at others;

so prone to judging, so severe at reproving;

so joyful in prosperity, so weak in adversity;

so often making many good resolutions and bringing them to so little effect.

3. When you have confessed and bewailed these and your other shortcomings with sorrow and sore displeasure at your own infirmity, make a firm resolution of continual amendment of your life and of your progress in all that is good. Then with full resignation and with your entire will, offer yourself to the honor of My name on the altar of your heart as a perpetual whole burnt-offering, even by faithfully presenting your body and soul to Me, to the end that you may be accounted worthy to draw near to offer this sacrifice of praise and thanksgiving to God, and to receive the Sacrament of My Body and Blood to your soul's health.

For there is no oblation worthier, no satisfaction greater for the destroying of sin, than that you offer yourself to God purely and entirely with the oblation of the Body and Blood of Christ in Holy Communion. If you have done what lies in you and are truly repent, then you may draw close to Me for pardon and grace often. As I live, says the Lord, I take no pleasure in the death of a sinner, but rather that you should be converted, and live. All your transgressions you have committed shall not be mentioned (Ez 18:22, 23).

8

———————

THE OBLATION OF CHRIST ON THE CROSS AND RESIGNATION OF THE SELF

hapter Focus: When we receive our Lord in the Blessed Sacrament, we should allow Him to change us, to mold us into His Disciple.

I once had a realistic dream where I was in the place of Dismas, the Good Thief, on the cross next to Jesus. He looked at me and asked me: "Why can't you love Me? Isn't this enough for you? I'm sacrificing My Body and Blood so that you can be with Me." My response was the same as Dismas - "Jesus, remember me, when You come into Your Kingdom." And He promised me that I would go to Paradise with Him that day. In my dream, I allowed Jesus' love to change me. The Fictional Narrative that follows the main part of this book discusses Dismas in some detail. (See also, Book III, Ch 57).

In the same way, it does us no good to receive Holy Communion, even while mindful of such an extraordinary blessing, and return from the Altar unchanged. Where is the meaning in that? Which is not to say that we don't wander through periods of distraction. Like Dismas, we have to empty ourselves of sin and accept God's gift; filling our emptiness with Christ's sacrifice. In this passage, Thomas uses the Voice of Christ to call us to join Him at the Cross with our emptiness. We bring nothing to the Altar but our empty selves. And our sins.

Remember in Chapter 7, when the Voice of the Beloved asks us to offer our selves as a perpetual offering to Jesus on the altars of our hearts? He says to do that with full resignation of our entire will. Chapter 8 brings us to that point. We need to imitate Christ by freely offering our empty selves to God the Father and our Lord Jesus Christ with our whole heart.

Nothing else will do.

~

CHAPTER 8, In Short.

1. Because Christ offered Himself on the Cross to God the Father for our sins, we also ought to offer ourselves to Him daily.

2. Offer yourself to Christ, and give yourself fully to God, in order that your offering may be accepted.

~

SCRIPTURE MEMORY PRAYER: "[E]very one of you who does not renounce all your possessions cannot be My Disciple." (Luke 14:33).

Question: Have you offered yourself to Jesus with all your heart?

Key Quote: Whatever you give except yourself is meaningless to Me; for I do not seek your gift, but you.

~

THE TEXT OF CHAPTER 8:

The Oblation Of Christ Upon The Cross and Resignation of the Self.

The Voice of the Beloved: Of My Own will I offered Myself to God the Father on the Cross for your sins with outstretched hands and naked body, so that nothing remained in Me that did not become fully a sacrifice for the Divine propitiation. So you also ought to offer yourself willingly every day to Me for a pure and holy oblation with all your strength and affections, even to the utmost powers of your heart. What more do I require of you than that you study to resign yourself completely to Me? **Whatever you give except yourself is meaningless to Me; for I do not seek your gift, but you.**

2. As it would not be sufficient for you even if you had all things except Me, so that whatever you would give to Me, even if you do not give Me yourself, cannot please Me. Offer yourself to Me, and give yourself fully to God, so your offering will be accepted. Behold I offered Myself fully to the Father for you. I gave My whole body and blood for food, that you might remain altogether Mine and I yours. But if you stand in yourself, and do not offer yourself freely to My will, your offering is not perfect, and neither will the union between us be complete.

Therefore if you will attain liberty and grace, the freewill offering of yourself into the hands of God ought to go before all your works. For this is the cause that so few are inwardly enlightened and made free, that they do not know how to deny themselves entirely. My word stands sure: "In the same way, every one of you who does not renounce all your possessions cannot be My Disciple (Lk 14:33)." You therefore, if you wish to be My Disciple, offer yourself to Me with all your heart.

9

___

WE SHOULD OFFER OURSELVES AND WHAT IS OURS TO GOD, AND PRAY FOR ALL

Chapter Focus: Do you remember your first sin? Or maybe what you confessed at your First Reconciliation? I don't remember. Neither does God.

When I drive through the neighborhood in which I grew up, I pray backward in time for that little boy - the seven year old me, who was so good at lying to his parents, cheating at school, stealing candy from the gas station, or just being downright honery (See Ch 2 focus). Those stains remain fifty-plus years later. And yes I know I've been forgiven. No doubt I confessed these sins to Monsignor Dirksen or Fr. O'Shea. But I remember these fine priests taking my confession very seriously. Just as my confessor does now.

Monsignor Dirksen would often tell me: "For your Penance, say you are sorry to your friend, give the value of what you stole to the poor if you can't restore it to the owner, and do something nice for your parents. But I want you to pray - oh won't you please pray the Lord's prayer - slowly and with heart. You must take care of your immortal soul. God's mercy is great. And He wants you to be clean and pure and holy, so that you can receive Him at Holy Communion, and be with Him in Heaven."

So off I would go. I usually did everything he asked of me. But when I would pray the Lord's Prayer, I'm sure I rushed. Thomas wants us to slow down and not rush through our prayers, especially as we ready ourselves for Holy Communion. He wants us to receive the forgiveness that is embedded in the Sacrament.

Thomas brings his particular petitions directly to the altar, since the precious Body and Blood of the Lord is the embodiment of the ultimate prayer. We are called to a prayerful purpose in receiving the Eucharist. We don't receive from habit but from privilege. We ingest the prayer. We take Him into our very body and sanctify our prayers to Him by ingesting His Presence, which chases out the residue of sin.

Thomas turns his focus toward shredding his sinfulness with Christ's holiness, recognizing that the only thing to do with his sins is to confess the sin, be sorry, and repent. He tells us that performing good deeds has little or no effect except as a means of penance: we learn by doing. Thomas knows that God will forgive him outright, and, in a way, this makes things worse because Thomas does not want to presume upon God's Mercy. Thomas ends the meditation by bringing the petitions of his family and friends to the altar. He wholeheartedly prays for his enemies, and, like in the Lord's prayer, asks to be forgiven to the extent that he committed acts or omissions of which he was unaware.

As my fifth grade teacher, Sr. Mary Luke would often pray, "My Jesus, Mercy!"

CHAPTER 9, In Short.

1. The Lord possesses everything in the heavens and the earth.

2. Lord, let your fiery love consume all my sins and offenses.

3. What can I do concerning my sins, except to confess and lament and pray for Your redemption?

4. I offer to You all my goodness, imperfect as it is, so that You may sanctify it.

5. I offer to You all the pious desires of Your devout followers: especially my family and friends.

6. I offer prayers to You especially for those who have injured me.

~

SCRIPTURE MEMORY PRAYER: "For all in Heaven and on earth is Yours; Yours, Lord, is kingship; You are exalted as Head over all." (1 Chronicles 29:11).

Question: How deep is God's Mercy? Are you letting Him apply His rich Mercy to your shortcomings and sins?

Key Quote: Behold, I commit myself to Your mercy, I resign myself to Your hands.

~

THE TEXT OF CHAPTER 9:

We Should Offer Ourselves and What is Ours to God, and to Pray for All.

The Disciple: Lord, all that is in the heavens and on the earth is Yours (1 Chr 29:11). I desire to offer myself up to You as a freewill offering, and to continue as Yours forever. Lord, in the uprightness of my heart I willingly offer myself to You today to be Your servant forever, in humble submission and for a sacrifice of perpetual praise (1 Chr 29:17). Receive me along with this Holy Communion of Your precious Body, which I celebrate before You this day in the presence of the Angels invisibly surrounding me, that it may be for the salvation of me and of all Your people.

2. Lord, I lay before You at this celebration all my sins and offenses which I have committed before You and Your holy Angels, from the day when I was first able to sin up to this hour; that You may consume and burn these sins - every one - with Your fiery love, and may do away with all the stains of my sins, and cleanse my

conscience from all my offenses, and restore me to Your favor which I have lost by sinning, fully forgiving me, and mercifully admitting me to the kiss of peace.

3. What can I do concerning my sins, except to humbly confess and lament these faults and unceasingly plead for Your redemption? O my God, I beseech You, be favorable to me and hear me when I stand before You. My sins severely displease me: I will never commit them again. But I grieve for my sins and will grieve so long as I live, truly repenting without wavering, and to make restitution as far as I can. Forgive me, O God, forgive me my sins for the sake of Your holy Name. Save my soul, which You have redeemed with Your precious blood. **Behold, I commit myself to Your mercy, I resign myself to Your hands.** Deal with me according to Your loving-kindness, not according to my wickedness and iniquity.

4. I also offer to You all my goodness, though it is barely noticeable and quite imperfect, that You may mend and sanctify it, that You may make it well pleasing and acceptable in Your sight, and draw it on forever towards perfection. Furthermore, bring me safely to a happy and blessed end despite my being a slothful and useless creature.

5. Moreover, I offer to You all the pious desires of Your devoted ones, the necessities of parents, friends, brothers, sisters, and all who are dear to me, and of those who have done good to me, or to others, for Your love. And for those who have desired and sought my prayers for themselves and all belonging to them, that all may feel themselves assisted by Your grace, enriched by Your consolation, protected from dangers, and freed from pains. And that in being delivered from all evils they may joyfully give abundant thanks to You.

6. I also offer to You prayers and Sacramental intercessions especially for those who have injured me in any way, or made me sad, or spoken evil concerning me, or have caused me any loss or displeasure. I likewise pray for all those whom I have at any time made sad, disturbed, burdened, and scandalized, by words or deeds, knowingly or ignorantly; that to all of us alike, You may equally pardon our sins and mutual offenses. O Lord take away from our hearts all suspicion,

indignation, anger, and contention, and whatever is able to injure charity and diminish brotherly love. Have mercy, Lord. Have mercy, Lord, on those who ask for Your mercy. Give grace to the needy, and make us such that we may be worthy to enjoy Your grace, and go forward to eternal life. Amen.

10

HOLY COMMUNION IS NOT TO BE OMITTED LIGHTLY

Chapter Focus: One summer Saturday afternoon, I was at the cabin, working on the orchard. That morning I recited my prayers and also read the Mass readings for Sunday. It was now about two o'clock: I had just finished mulching and was just enjoying the breeze when I recognized the time. I didn't want to go anywhere, but knew that if I put away the tractor and drove home and took a quick shower, I could make it to Confession (Reconciliation). Or, I could probably skip Confession, take a nap in the hammock, and complain about the bugs, but I really do not like to miss taking Holy Communion on Sundays. So I put away the tractor and closed the cabin. I had some stain on my soul, in one of those sin areas where I wasn't sure whether to make a Confession of it or not. But I didn't want to receive Holy Communion until my question was resolved. So, my resolution was to go to Confession so that I could receive the Blessed Sacrament at Sunday Mass.

It's easy to make excuses on why we should omit receiving Holy Communion. Sometimes, it's a need to go to Confession. Or maybe you're that person who has to eat something as you are walking out the door to Mass instead of fasting for one hour before Mass because you want to sleep in. I'm raising my hand here. Our Lord tells us to come to the table. He wants us hungry when we arrive. While we may not feel worthy to receive Him and attend His banquet, we should not put on a false sense of humility. Jesus has given us permission - invited us to receive Him, so put aside such excuses and exercise some discipline. If mortal sin afflicts us, we should seek out the remedy of Confession. In developing good habits and discarding the bad, and in making use of the Sacrament of Reconciliation, we can approach Him and receive Him (Jn 14:23). We can attend His banquet.

Now go wash up and put on your Sunday best, the Prince of Peace is opening His doors!

CHAPTER 10, In Short.

1. To obtain healing, take yourself to the Fountain of grace and divine mercy.

2. The devout suffer more from Satan's evil suggestions while preparing for Holy Communion.

3. Too much anxiety hinders you from obtaining devotion.

4. How does it help you to put off confession of your sins for a long time, or to defer Holy Communion?

5. Those who put off Holy Communion lightly have very little love.

6. When hindered from receiving Communion, the Disciple still intends to receive; and so shall not lack the fruit of the Sacrament.

7. Whoever prepares to receive Communion only when a festival is at hand or when custom demands it, will often be unprepared for its arrival.

SCRIPTURE MEMORY PRAYER: "Whoever loves Me will keep My word, and My Father will love him, and We will come to him and make Our dwelling with him." (John 14:23).

Question: How does it help you to put off the confession of your sins for a long time, or to defer Holy Communion?

Key Quote: Do not neglect Holy Communion because of some little vexation or trouble, but rather confess it, and forgive freely all offenses committed against you.

~

THE TEXT OF CHAPTER 10:

Holy Communion is not to be Omitted Lightly.

The Voice of the Beloved: Take yourself frequently to the Fountain of grace and divine mercy, to the Fountain of goodness and all purity; so that in the end you may obtain the healing of your passions and vices, and may be made stronger and more watchful against all temptations and the wiles of the devil. The enemy, so far as he can, knows of the strong, beneficial and powerful remedy that lies with reception of Holy Communion. The devil therefore strives by all means and occasions to draw back and hinder the faithful and devout.

2. When some set about to prepare themselves for Holy Communion, they suffer more from the evil suggestions of Satan. The evil spirit himself (as is written in Job), comes among the sons of God that he may trouble them by his accustomed evil dealings, or make them timid and perplexed; with the intent that he may diminish their affections, or take away their faith by his attacks, if by chance he may prevail upon them to give up Holy Communion altogether, or to come to the Sacrament with lukewarm hearts. No matter how wicked and terrible his wiles may be, his delusions must not be heeded, but rather cast back upon his own head. The wretch must be despised and laughed to scorn: neither must Holy Communion be omitted because of his insults and the inward troubles which he stirs up.

3. Often too much carefulness or anxiety or other moving confession hinders you from obtaining devotion. Act according to the

counsel of the wise, and lay aside your anxiety and scruple, because it hinders the grace of God and destroys the devotion of your mind. **Do not neglect Holy Communion because of some little vexation or trouble, but rather confess it, and forgive freely all offenses committed against you.** And if you have offended any one, humbly beg for pardon, and God shall freely forgive you.

4. What does it profit you to put off the confession of your sins for a long time, or to defer Holy Communion? Cleanse yourself now. Spit out the poison with all speed, having to take the remedy, and you shall feel yourself better than if you deferred it a long time. If today you defer it on one account, tomorrow perhaps some greater obstacle will come, and so you may be a long time hindered from Communion and become more unfit. As soon as you can, shake yourself from your present heaviness and sloth, for it profits nothing to be anxious so long, to go far on your way with a heaviness of heart, and because of daily little obstacles to sever yourself from divine things: it is hurtful to defer your Communion long, for this commonly brings on great torpor. Alas! there are some who are lukewarm and undisciplined, who willingly find excuses for delaying repentance, and desire to defer Holy Communion, so that they should be bound to keep a strict watch on themselves.

5. Alas! they who have put off Holy Communion so lightly have little charity, and a flagging devotion. How happy is the one, how acceptable to God, who lives and stays in such purity of conscience, that any day he could be ready and well disposed to communicate, if it were in his power, and this might be done without the notice of others. If a Disciple sometimes abstains for the sake of humility or some sound cause, he is to be commended for his reverence. But if drowsiness has taken hold of him, he ought to rouse himself and do what lies in him; and the Lord will help his desire for the good will which he has, which God specially approves.

6. When hindered by sufficient cause, a Disciple will still practice good will and pious intentions to communicate; and so shall not be lacking in the fruit of the Sacrament. For every day and every hour

the devout Disciple is able to draw near to spiritual communion* with Christ to his soul's health and without hindrance.

Nevertheless on certain days and at the appointed time he ought to receive the Body and Blood of his Redeemer with affectionate reverence, and should seek after the praise and honor of God, instead of his own comfort. For so often does he communicate mystically, and is invisibly refreshed, as he devoutly calls to mind the mystery of Christ's incarnation and His Passion, and is inflamed with the love of Him.

7. Whoever prepares to receive Communion only when a festival is at hand or when custom demands it, will too often be unprepared. Blessed is the one who offers himself to God for a whole burnt-offering, so often as he celebrates or communicates! Do not be too slow nor too hurried in your celebrating, but preserve the good custom received from those with whom you live. You ought not to produce weariness and annoyance in others, but observe the received custom, according to the institution of the elders; and to minister to the profit of others rather than to your own devotion or feeling.

*An Act of Spiritual Communion

My Jesus,
I believe that You are present in the Most Holy Sacrament.
I love You above all things,
and I desire to receive You into my soul.
Since I cannot at this moment receive You sacramentally,
come at least spiritually into my heart.
I embrace You as if You were already there
and unite myself wholly to You.
Never permit me to be separated from You.
Amen.

11

THE MOST NECESSARY NOURISHMENT TO A FAITHFUL SOUL ARE THE BODY AND BLOOD OF CHRIST AND THE HOLY SCRIPTURES

Chapter Focus: Have you ever been invited to a party and wondered if it's a mistake?

For Donna and me, with our seven children, we were often excluded from events, since we are our own party. Our go to social event was usually to throw a potluck and invite other big families!

Imagine my surprise whenever our family was <u>actually</u> invited to a party, or a wedding or anywhere. Our kids are grown now, but we always make a point to invite young, large families, to our picnics and potlucks. Pulled pork, hot dogs, and sheet cake go a long way toward filling tummies.

These days things are different, but I still find myself double checking invites to make sure the envelope or email didn't arrive at our house by mistake. For example, we were recently surprised to be invited to an event. I called my host just to make sure he hadn't invited us by mistake...to save him (and us) the embarrassment of explaining why we were appearing on his doorstep. "Oh yes," he said, "bring the whole family! I'm really looking forward to you coming to the party. I think you'll like some of my friends. We're just going to break bread ... ahem... hot dog buns, that is, and maybe sing some songs and tell stories around the campfire." Perhaps he knows that we are practically empty-nesters at this point. Or perhaps he didn't know, and was just being generous and genuinely wanted us at the party. Regardless, I was pleased, and we had a wonderful time.

Jesus treats us with genuine generosity when He invites us to the table of Plenty. He wants everyone to come, to eat, to drink, to celebrate. There's always enough to go around. Like a good Host, along the way He makes sure we are introduced to His friends, the Saints, and checks to see if we are comfortable. We may even sing a few songs and listen to some great stories.

Thomas a'Kempis expresses a similar wonder at our Lord's open Hands and graciousness as he describes being invited to Christ's banquet. The core of Chapter 11 lies in paragraph 4, where Thomas says that he only needs two things: Food and Light. He then states that his food is the Body of Christ, his light the Word of God. What a privilege!

One more thing: Watermelon tastes better when it's cut into small wedges.

A SPECIAL NOTE to Priests and Deacons (David, Jeff, Thomas, John, Patrick, Greg, Jim; and all the others over the years); and to my other Christian Pastors (especially Marie, Don, Eric, Mary Jean, Gary) on the Feast of The Good Shepherd:

Thank you for saying "Yes" to God's call. We thank you for leading us and making Holy worship possible for us. You can be many things, but mostly, we want you to be a holy example for us. Not in extreme severe piety, but humble joyful piety. Help us to find God's grace and mercy. Teach us to pray. Teach us to grow closer to God. When you treat us as your beloved children, we will honor you as our spiritual leaders. We know you bear a great responsibility in celebrating the Mass, or leading worship; in being accountable for the souls in your charge. Let us help you by holding up your arms during the battles when you are tired (Ex 17:12). Finally, it's okay to smile, laugh and be joyful, like our parents were (or what we wished they had been). Taking the role of our kind-hearted, wisdom-filled parent will do just fine. That said, it's okay to be tough-minded and candid with us from the pulpit - there's a big difference between being tough-minded and severe. We look to you, like we look to Jesus, to open our minds to the Scriptures (Lk 24:45). Amen.

CHAPTER 11, In Short.

1. Great is the blessedness of the devout soul that shares in Your banquet.

2. Jesus is considerate of our weakness in that He hides Himself under the Sacrament.

3. If you never see the Lord in His own Glory, everything which you see and hear in this world should count as nothing.

4. There are two things necessary in this life: God's Sacred Body and His Holy Word.

5. We give thanks to God for those holy doctrines furnished to us by the Prophets and Apostles.

6. <u>For priests</u>: Great and honorable is your office in that you are given to consecrate the Sacrament of the Lord.

7. <u>For priests</u>: To priests is it specially said in the Law, "Be holy, for I, the Lord your God, Am holy."

8. <u>For priests</u>: Assist us with Your grace, O Almighty God, to converse worthily and devoutly with You.

SCRIPTURE MEMORY PRAYER: "[B]lessed is the one who takes no offense at Me." (Luke 7:23).

Question: What is the light of your soul - your Bread of Life?

Key Quote: For the Word of God is the light of my soul, and Your Sacrament the Bread of Life.

~

The Most Necessary Nourishment to a Faithful Soul Are the Body and Blood of Christ and the Holy Scriptures.

The Disciple: O sweetest Lord Jesus, how great is the blessedness of the devout soul that feeds with You in Your banquet. There, set before that soul, is no other food than Yourself the only Beloved. You are more to be desired than all the desires of the heart. And to me indeed it would be sweet to pour forth my tears in Your presence from the very bottom of my heart, and with the devout Magdalene to water Your feet with my tears (Lk 7:38). But where is this devotion? Where is this outpouring of holy tears? Surely in Your presence and in the presence of the holy Angels my whole heart ought to burn and weep for joy. For are You truly present in the Eucharist, although hidden under another form.

2. For my eyes could not endure to behold You in Your own Divine brightness, neither could the whole world stand before the splendor of the glory of Your Majesty. In this, therefore, You are considerate of my weakness, in that You hide Yourself under the Sacrament. I truly possess and adore Him Whom the Angels adore in Heaven - but I as yet by faith, the Angels by sight and without a veil (2 Cor 3:12-18). I must be content with the light of true faith, and to walk internally until the day of eternal brightness dawns, and the shadows of figures pass away (Songs 2:17).

But when that which is perfect comes, the use of Sacraments shall cease, because the Blessed in Heavenly glory have no need of the medicine of the Sacramental remedy. For they rejoice unceasingly in the presence of God, beholding His glory face to face, and being changed from glory to glory of the infinite God, they taste the Word of God made flesh, as He was in the beginning, is now, and will be forever (2 Cor 3:18, 1 Cor 13:9-12; Jn 1:14).

3. When I think on these wondrous things, even spiritual comfort

becomes a weariness to me. For so long as I do not openly see my Lord in His own Glory, I count as nothing everything I see and hear in this world. You, O God, are my Witness that nothing is able to comfort me, no creature is able to give me rest except You, O my God, Whom I desire to contemplate forever. But this is not possible, so long as I remain in this mortal state. Therefore I must set myself to great patience, and submit every desire of mine to You.

For even Your Saints, O Lord, who now rejoice with You in the kingdom of Heaven, waited for the coming of Your glory while they lived here in faith and great glory. What they believed, I believe; what they hoped for, I hope for; whatever role they have attained, through the same manner and with Your grace, I hope to attain (Ruth 1:16). Meanwhile, I will walk in faith, strengthened by the examples of the Saints. I will also have holy books for comfort and for a mirror of life, and above these all Your most holy Body and Blood shall be for me a special remedy and refuge.

4. I find that in this life there are two things I feel are necessary to me - without which this miserable life would be intolerable to me: Being detained in my bodily prison, I confess that I need two things, namely food and light. You have therefore given to me who am so weak, Your sacred Body and Blood, for the refreshing of my soul and body, and have set Your Word for a lamp to my feet (Ps 119:105). Without these two I could not live properly. **For the Word of God is the light of my soul, and Your Sacrament the Bread of Life** (Jn 6:35). These may also be called the two tables, placed on either side in the storehouse of Your Holy Church. One table is that of the Sacred Altar, bearing the holy Bread, that is the precious Body and Blood of Christ. The other is the table of the Divine Law, containing holy doctrine, teaching the true faith, and leading steadfastly onward even to that which is within the veil, where the Holy of Holies rests.

5. Thanks be to You, O Lord Jesus, Light of Light everlasting, for that table of holy doctrine which You have furnished to us by Your servants the Prophets and Apostles and other teachers. Thanks be to You, O Creator and Redeemer of all, Who to make known Your love to the whole world has prepared a great supper, in which You have

set forth for good not the typical lamb, but Your most Holy Body and Blood (Lk 22:14-20). You have made all Your faithful ones joyful with this holy banquet and gave them the cup of salvation to drink, where all the delights of Paradise reside, and the holy Angels feast with us, and yet with a happier sweetness (Ps 23:5).

6. Oh how great and honorable is the office of the Priest, to whom it is given to consecrate the Sacrament of the Lord of Majesty with holy words, to bless it with the lips, to hold the Host in their hands, to receive the Cup with their own mouths, and to administer it to others! Oh how clean those hands ought to be, how pure the mouth, how holy the body, how unspotted the heart of the Priest, to whom so often the Author of purity enters in! From the mouth of the Priest nothing ought to proceed but that which is holy, what is honest and profitable, because he so often receives the Sacrament of Christ.

7. His eyes ought to be single and pure, since these eyes are accustomed to looking upon the Body of Christ. His hands should be pure and lifted towards Heaven, which regularly hold within them the Creator of Heaven and earth. It is especially said to Priests in the Law, "Be holy, for I, the Lord your God, Am holy (Lv 19:2)."

8. Assist us with Your grace, O Almighty God, that we who have taken upon us the Priestly office, may be able to speak worthily and devoutly with You in all purity and good conscience (1 Tim 1:5). And if we are not able to have our conversation in such innocence of life as we ought, still grant to us to worthily lament the sins which we have committed, and in the spirit of humility and full purpose of a good will, to serve You more earnestly for the future.

12

THOSE ABOUT TO COMMUNICATE WITH CHRIST SHOULD PREPARE TO RECEIVE HIM WITH GREAT DILIGENCE

Chapter Focus: A few weeks ago my cousin, Roger, came for a visit. I was glad to receive and host him as we are good friends. He also asked if Donna and I could open our house to the other cousins who lived in our area. "Sure," I said, "we'd be happy to host. It'll be fun." Donna and I then proceeded to clean the house: dusting, taking out the trash, vacuuming, washing windows, shaking out rugs, putting away (or hiding) the junk and clutter. We added extra chairs, donned table cloths to the tables and banished our rickety furniture to the garage. We wanted our guests to be comfortable and to present a clean house as a way to honor this rare gathering. Soon the door bell rang and we stopped cleaning and began hosting. Everyone had a good time. No one mentioned how clean everything was, or asked about the mysterious, blanket-covered piles in the garage.

Just as you would clean your house before guests arrive, so you should prepare yourself before receiving Christ. Of course, as with the guest preparation, it's never enough. Just as our guests didn't comment on our piles of hidden junk out of politeness, Jesus does likewise. He overlooks our sins, smiles at our attempts to hide the junk and unsightly baggage we push to our dark places. Just as He is a consummate Host (Ch 11), He is also a gracious Guest. In His mercy, He asks us to open the door of our hearts and receive Him. He always brings the best Bread and the choicest Wine.

When we receive the Blessed Sacrament, we are taking Jesus into the house of our body. Therefore, we should receive Him with faith, hope, and charity (1 Cor 13). In receiving this Sacrament, we open ourselves to His grace and abundant life (Jn 10:10). As with guests in our home, we grow closer to Christ by sharing His meal - the meal of Himself. When Jesus invites Himself into our house, like Zacchaeus, we receive salvation and joy and become inspired to repair our injustices four times over - even after He leaves (Lk 19:1-10).

CHAPTER 12, In Short.

1. Christ seeks pure hearts as a place to rest and to sanctify.

2. You cannot prepare enough to receive Christ based upon your merits, but only by His tenderness and grace.

3. When Christ bestows the grace of devotion upon you, give thanks to God, because He has shown you mercy.

4. You ought to prepare yourself for devotion both before and after Holy Communion.

SCRIPTURE MEMORY PRAYER: "I came that you might have life, and have it more abundantly." (John 10:10).

Question: Will you follow our Lord's command to come and receive? Will you answer His request (His plea!) to enter into your house?

Key Quote: Come and receive Me.

THE TEXT OF CHAPTER 12:

Those about to Communicate with Christ Should Prepare to Receive Him with Great Diligence.

The Voice of the Beloved: "I am the Lover of purity and Giver of sanctity. I seek a pure heart, the place of My rest is there. Prepare for Me a large furnished upper room, and I will eat the Passover at your house, together with My Disciples (Mk 14:14-15).

"If it is your will that I come to you and abide with you, purge out the old leaven, and cleanse the living space of your heart (1 Cor 5:7). Shut out the whole world and the throng of your vices. Sit as a sparrow alone upon the house-top, and think of your own excesses with soulful bitterness (Ps 102:7).

"For every lover prepares the best and fairest place for their Beloved, in order to make known the affection of those which entertain the Beloved.

2. "Yet know that that you cannot make sufficient preparation out of the merit of any of your actions even if you prepared yourself for a whole year and even if you thought of nothing else. But only out of My tenderness and grace are you permitted to draw close to My table; as though a beggar was called to a rich man's dinner, and had no other payment to offer for the benefits done to him than to humble himself and give him thanks. Therefore, do as much as what lies within you, and do it diligently, not from custom or of necessity, but with fear, reverence, and affection, receive the Body of Your Beloved Lord God, Who promises to come to you. I Am He Who has called you. I commanded it to be done. I will supply to you what is lacking. **Come and receive Me.**

3. "Give thanks to God when I bestow the grace of devotion; not because you are worthy, but because I have had mercy on you.

"If you have no devotion, but rather feel dry, persist in prayer, sigh and knock (Mt 7:7). Do not stop praying until you prevail in obtaining some crumb or drop of saving grace. You have need of Me, but I have no need of you. Nor do you come to sanctify Me, but I come to sanctify you and make you better. You come that you may be sanctified by Me, and be united to Me - that you may receive fresh grace, and be enkindled to amend your life anew. See that you do not neglect this grace, but prepare your heart with all diligence and receive Your Beloved.

4. "Prepare yourself for devotion not only before Communion, but also keep yourself, with all diligence, in such a state after receiving the Sacrament. Nor is less watchfulness needed afterward than devout preparation beforehand: for strict watchfulness afterward becomes, in turn, the best preparation for gaining more grace. For if you immediately return from Communion and give yourself up to exterior consolations, you are made entirely indisposed to good. Beware of speaking too much; remain in secret, and enjoy communion with your God; for You have Him Whom the whole world cannot take away from you.

"I Am He to Whom you ought to give your whole self; so that from now on you may live not in yourself, but in Me, free from all anxiety."

13

THE DEVOUT SOUL YEARNS WITH THEIR WHOLE HEART FOR UNION WITH CHRIST

Chapter Focus: What is the desire of Thomas' heart ? Unity with God; and Thomas finds that unity via the Blessed Sacrament.

I remember as a child attending First Communion class, and Sister Mary Zachary handed us each an unconsecrated host: unleavened bread which would be used for Communion Hosts, "Remember, children," said Sister Mary Zachary, "these have not be blessed, so you are not really receiving Jesus' Body right now. But when you receive Jesus, just say a prayer to Him in your Head; something like 'Bless me and my family, Lord.' Just like you were asking a favor of a friend." A few weeks later, wearing an ill-fitting hand-me-down jacket and well worn collared shirt with a clip-on black tie, I received the real Jesus in the real, consecrated Host. It was a day of celebration, uniting my heart to God's Heart.

Over the years my approach to the Blessed Sacrament has morphed from wonder to withdrawal to entitlement to prayerful reception. These days I tend to offer my Holy Communion for the benefit of others in my life - to unite my prayer with theirs in petitioning God's blessing, mercy, healing, forgiveness, and gratitude. I am again in wonder that God lets me unite my prayer with His blessing.

In yearning to receive Holy Communion, Thomas likens his prayer in receiving Communion to a dinner conversation with an intimate Friend. He prays for this continued intimacy. Thomas continues to bow down in worship before this God Who doesn't huddle up with the rich and powerful, but with the simple and humble: God hides Himself from the worldly but readily reveals Himself to all seekers even as He seeks them. Thomas concludes his prayer of praise and thanksgiving by telling God that the only gift we can bring to Him is our heart. This side of Heaven we act on this giving process by approaching the altar to receive Him in Holy Communion. We receive Him. We give to Him. He fulfills this prayer request by condescending to come to us in the form of Bread and Wine.

While the whole Chapter is itself a prayer, Thomas concludes with ecstatic praise, well worth repeating before you receive Holy Communion.

CHAPTER 13, In Short.

1. Pray to be wholly united to God by means of Holy Communion.

2. God is truly my Beloved, in Whom my soul delights to dwell upon all the days of my life.

3. What creature is so beloved under Heaven as the devout soul to which God enters, that He may feed it with His glorious flesh?

SCRIPTURE MEMORY PRAYER: "My Beloved is radiant and ruddy; outstanding among thousands." (Song of Songs 5:10).

Question: Do I acknowledge Christ's Presence in the Blessed Sacrament regularly and with prayerful humility?

Key Quote: You are truly a God that hides Yourself, and Your counsel is not with the wicked, but Your Word is with the humble and the simple.

~

The Text of Chapter 13:

The Devout Soul Yearns for Union with Christ with Their Whole Heart.

The Disciple: Who will grant to me, O Lord, that I may find You alone, and fully open my heart to You, and enjoy You as much as my soul desires? And from now on may people not look upon me, nor any creature influence me or even have regard for me, but that You alone speak to me and I to You, even as one's beloved speaks to their beloved, and friend to a friend at dinner?

For this I pray, and for this I long: that I may be wholly united to You, and may withdraw my heart from all created things. May I learn more and more to relish Heavenly and eternal things by way of Holy Communion and frequent celebration. Ah, Lord God, when will I be entirely united and lost in You, and altogether forgetful of myself? You in me, and I in You (Jn 15:4). Even so grant us both in like manner to continue together in one.

2. You are truly my Beloved, the choicest among ten thousand, in Whom my soul delights to dwell upon all the days of her life (Songs 5:10). You are truly my Peacemaker, in Whom is perfect peace and true rest, apart from Whom is labor and sorrow and infinite misery. **You are truly a God that hides Yourself, and Your counsel is not with the wicked, but Your Word is with the humble and the simple.**

O how sweet is Your Spirit, O Lord! Who, to show Your sweetness towards Your children, promises to refresh them with the Bread which is full of sweetness, Bread which comes down from Heaven.

Truly, no other nation is so great which has its gods drawing so near to them as You, our God, draw near to all Your faithful ones, to

Whom for their daily comfort, and for lifting up their heart to Heaven You give Yourself for their food and delight (Dt 4:7).

3. For what other nation is there so renowned as the Christian people? Or what creature is so beloved under Heaven as the devout soul to which God enters, that He may feed it with His glorious flesh?

PRAYER

O unspeakable grace! O wonderful condescension! O immeasurable love specially bestowed upon we, Your people! But what reward shall I give to the Lord for this grace, for a love so mighty? There is nothing which I am able to present more acceptable than to give my heart completely to God and closely unite it to Him. Then all that is within me will rejoice, and my soul shall be perfectly united to God. Then shall He say to me, "If You will be with Me, I will be with You." And I will answer Him, "Promise, O Lord, to abide with me, I will gladly be with You; this is my whole desire, even that my heart be united to You."

14

A DEVOUT PERSON'S FERVENT DESIRE TOWARD RECEIVING THE BODY AND BLOOD OF CHRIST

Chapter Focus: Thomas reflects deeply on receiving Holy Communion. Two pictures returned to my mind from Chapter 1: First, the elderly woman at Mass who struggles to her feet, with a tentative grip on her walker, dragging her gnarled, arthritic body to the aisle to receive the Body of Christ. Second, the elementary school boys and girls, lined up in their First Communion formal clothes, eager to receive Our Lord, like a bride her Bridegroom. The first receives Him as medicine or Bread for the journey. The second receive Him for the first time in innocence and awe, in purity and charity. These witnesses inspire me. These Disciples awaken in me a sense for the sort of devotion I need to tap into so that I may recognize the Holiness presented to me, and the privilege I am about to receive without cost.

In the second paragraph of this chapter, Thomas composes a prayer for us as an aid to cultivate a desire for receiving Holy Communion devoutly. Thomas ends with a confession that he's not as fervent as he'd like to be. Me too. But Thomas knows that our Lord may grant such fervency as a consolation in His good time, putting in us the desire and the innocence to receive worthily.

Take advantage of His powerful Mercy today!

CHAPTER 14, In Short.

1. When I call to mind how devout persons draw near to the Blessed Sacrament, they do so with the deepest devotion.

2. Truly ardent people of faith become a proof of Your Sacred Presence in the Breaking of the Bread.

3. God's Mercy is powerful enough to grant that longed for grace.

SCRIPTURE MEMORY PRAYER: "As the deer longs for streams of water, so my soul longs for You, O God." (Psalm 42:2).

Question: On a scale from 1 to 10, with 1 being indifferent, and 10 being ardent, how would you describe your level of desire when receiving Holy Communion?

Key Quote: Oh, the impressive ardent faith of these devout people; they demonstrate the very proof of Your Sacred Presence!

THE TEXT OF CHAPTER 14:

A Devout Person's Fervent Desire Toward Receiving the Body and Blood of Christ.

The Disciple: Ah, how great is the abundance of Your sweetness, O Lord, which You have laid up for those that fear You.

O Lord, when I call to mind how the devout draw near to Your Sacrament, they do so with the deepest devotion and affection. Very often I am confounded and blush for shame, because I approach Your altar and the Holy Communion table so carelessly and coldly. Likewise, I remain so dry and lacking in affection for You, in such a way that I am not wholly enkindled with love before You, my God, nor so vehemently drawn and affected like those devoted to You have demonstrated. These are the devout, who out of the earnest desire for Communion and tender affection of heart, could not refrain from weeping in receiving You, but as it were with mouth of heart and body alike they panted inwardly after You (Ps 42:2). O God, O Fountain of Life, they had no power to appease or satisfy their hunger, except by receiving Your Body with joyfulness and spiritual eagerness.

2. Oh, the impressive ardent faith of these devout people; they demonstrate the very proof of Your Sacred Presence! For they know their Lord in the breaking of the Bread, whose heart so strongly burns within them as when Jesus walked with the Disciples by the way (Lk 24:32). Ah me! for the most part such love and devotion as this is far from me. I lack this vehement love and ardor. Therefore, be merciful to me, O Jesus. Be good, sweet, and kind, and sometimes grant to Your poor Disciple the ability to feel, even just a little, the cordial affection of Your love in Holy Communion, so that my faith may grow stronger, my hope in Your goodness increase, and my charity, once kindled within me by the tasting of the Heavenly manna, may never fail (1 Cor 13:13).

3. Your Mercy is powerful indeed: Powerful enough to grant me the grace which I long for and to visit me most tenderly with the spirit of fervor on the day of Your good pleasure. For although I do not burn with desire as readily as those who are especially devoted towards You, yet, by Your grace, I ask to have this inflamed desire, praying and wishing that I be made partaker with all such fervent lovers of You and be numbered among their holy company.

15

GRACE OF DEVOTION IS ACQUIRED BY HUMILITY AND SELF-DENIAL

Chapter Focus: Thirsty. And a heat-stress warning posted at the entry to the bivouac site. I was so thirsty that summer day. Marching fifteen miles with a full pack and weapon in the South Carolina heat radiating up through the soles of my boots. My ill-sized helmet slopped around on my head from my sweat-slippery forehead and soaked temples. The adjustment strap had broken earlier in the bivouac and now I regretted not attending to it with some duct tape. It was like being slapped in the back of the neck every time Drill Sergeant Parnell called "Double Time!" - which meant we would start running. I was thankful that he was tired too. I was thankful for the Basic Training buzz hair cut. I was thankful I still had some water in my canteen. Thinking so, I reached for my canteen again. Just a swallow to get me through that last two miles. Warm water can make you puke, but it is still water. So I guzzled it down. My buddies were also empty or low. Some guys had fallen out of the march due to heat stress. When we reached our camp, Drill Sergeant Harris greeted us with encouragement and a water hose. He hosed us down like cars at a high school car wash and laughed at our sorry state of exhaustion. "C'mon Private, get in the fountain and get your soakin'! Rest up. You made it! Congratulations, soldier!

Big day tomorrow! Now get out your canteens and let's fill 'em up. Hey, dummies, you gotta take the caps off so the water can go in!" We all laughed at ourselves as we struggled to unscrew our canteen lids to fill our canteens. Then we walked into the splash and guzzled at the hose. Nothing mattered: I forgot about my helmet, my sweaty clothes, my sore feet. Of course we all had to do push-ups in the mud puddle, but didn't care. It washed off.

I never thought I'd compare Sergeant Harris to Jesus, but when Jesus encounters us thirsty and empty, He refreshes us. When He anoints us, we forget about our discomfort, our exhaustion, our petty annoyances. We can leave all that behind and enter into the moment of His abundant grace.

Seeking the grace needed for devotion is a task requiring patience and faith. When we wait on God, it is easy to lose heart and feel abandoned, like carrying a full pack and rifle on an endless summer march. But God chooses the time, place, and manner of his revelation to us, often to achieve maximum impact. His timing is perfect. Our seeking is imperfect. Our need for being filled is clear by the many vessels we carry with us: dry and empty. When He fills us, His anointing overflows with abundance.

Often, as Thomas points out, we are not ready for grace. God won't pour His oil into us when we've foolishly left the lids on our canteens. God waits for us to realize our mistakes. In our pride, we blame God even for our own mistakes. That's usually when He laughingly shows us that we need to unscrew the lid to our canteen, so it can be filled.

When we remove the obstacles to God's blessing, His oil of grace pours in unabated, overflowing. Receiving Him in Holy Communion is like that: Union with the Divine, made possible by setting aside our pride and selfishness.

So next time you are preparing your heart for receiving Jesus, get in the fountain and get your soakin'! Rest up. Ready your canteen by taking off the lid. Fill up! It's a big day tomorrow!

CHAPTER 15, In Short.

1. Seek the grace of devotion, and let God decide the time and manner of His Heavenly visitation.

2. If grace is always immediately given to you, you could hardly bear it.

3. Immediately after you have given yourself to God, you will be united and at peace in the Divine will.

4. The Disciple shall see his heart enlarged, because of the Hand of the Lord.

~

SCRIPTURE MEMORY PRAYER: "Then you shall see and be radiant, your heart shall throb and overflow." (Isaiah 60:5).

Question: How are you seeking the grace of devotion?

Key Quote: Where the Lord finds empty vessels, there He gives His blessing.

~

THE TEXT OF CHAPTER 15:

Grace of Devotion is Acquired by Humility and Self-Denial.

The Voice of the Beloved: You ought to seek earnestly the grace of devotion, to ask for it fervently, to wait for it patiently and faithfully, to receive it gratefully, to preserve it humbly, to work with it diligently, and leave to God the time and manner of Heavenly visitation until it comes. Chiefly you ought to humble yourself when you feel little or no devotion inwardly, yet don't be cast down too much, nor grieve out of measure. In one short moment God often gives what He has long denied. He sometimes gives at the end of prayer what at the beginning of prayer He has deferred.

2. If grace were always given immediately, and were at hand at

your wish, it would be hardly bearable to one so weak. The grace of devotion is to be waited upon with good hope and with humble patience. Yet when it is not given, or when it is mysteriously taken away, impute it to yourself and to your sins. It is sometimes a small thing which hinders and hides grace (if indeed that ought to be called small and not great, which hinders so great a good). But if you remove this obstacle, be it small or great, and perfectly overcome it, you will have what you asked for.

3. For immediately after you have given yourself to God with all your heart, and have sought neither this nor that according to your own will and pleasure, but have altogether settled yourself in Him, you shall find yourself united and at peace: nothing shall give you so sweet delight and relish as the good pleasure of the Divine will. Whoever therefore has lifted up his will to God with singleness of heart, and has delivered himself from every inordinate love or dislike of any created thing will be the most fit for receiving grace and worthy of the gift of devotion. **For where the Lord finds empty vessels, there He gives His blessing** (2 Kgs 4:1-7). And the more perfectly a Disciple forsakes things which are not beneficial, and the more he dies to himself, the more quickly grace comes, the more plentifully grace enters in, and the higher grace lifts up the free heart.

4. The Disciple shall then see, and flow together, and wonder, and his heart shall be enlarged within him, because the hand of the Lord is with him, and he has put himself wholly in His hands forever (Is 60:5). Lo, thus shall the Disciple be blessed that seeks God with all his heart, and receives not his soul in vain. This Disciple in receiving the Holy Eucharist obtains the great grace of Divine Union, because he has no regard for his own devotion and comfort, but above all devotion and comfort, to the glory and honor of God.

*N.B. FEEL free to substitute Chapter 14's Scripture Memory Prayer instead. "As the deer longs for streams of water, so my soul longs for You, O God." (Psalm 42:2).

16

LAYING OPEN OUR NECESSITIES TO CHRIST AND REQUIRING HIS GRACE

Chapter Focus: Imagine coming into your house on a cold, blustery day. You are snow-covered, wet, and chilled through your coat. But entering the door, you see the glow of a fire crackling in the fireplace. At first, when you stand in front of the fire, you simply want to warm up, take off the soggy clothes and revel in the warmth. The need for warmth has been fulfilled. With a cup of hot tea, the heat travels to your insides, which relax as your thirst for sustaining fluid settles in. However, when you linger too close to that fire, its heat is soaked up too fast, and then, if you stay too long, the heat becomes too much to absorb - it even becomes painful. For a minute, as the steam rises from your socks, you think you may go up in flames! You back off so as to not get burned, adjusting your distance until you get to the level of heat that is beneficial for you.

Thomas relates such a feeling in this Chapter, approaching our Lord closer and closer in Holy Communion. Our desire should be to burn up anything that is not of God. We have to get close enough to Him to let Him cauterize our sinful sores. The Disciple asks Jesus to enkindle him; to set him on fire with the love of the Holy Spirit, even to the point of being lost in the process. We need to approach again and again, until we are purified and gain the understanding needed to overcome our vices and promote our virtues. We do that through the intimacy of receiving Him in the form of Bread and Wine.

≈

CHAPTER 16, In Short.

1. Lord, You know my weaknesses and the necessities for which I suffer.

2. I stand poor and naked before You, requiring grace and imploring Your mercy.

3. If only You would kindle, consume, and transform me into Yourself!

≈

SCRIPTURE MEMORY PRAYER: "I raise my eyes toward the mountains." (Psalm 121:1).

Question: What necessities do you need to lay open to Christ?

Key Quote: Do not let me go away from You hungry and dry.

≈

THE TEXT OF CHAPTER 16:

Laying Open Our Necessities to Christ and Requiring His Grace.

The Disciple: O most sweet and loving Lord, Whom I now desire to receive devoutly, You know my weaknesses and the necessities for which I suffer, in what evils and vices I exist on. I am often weighed down, tempted, disturbed, and defiled with these. I come to You for remedy, I plead with You for consolation and support. I speak to You Who know all things, to Whom all my secrets are open and Who alone are able to perfectly comfort and help me. You know what good things I need most, and how poor I am in the virtues.

2. Behold, I stand poor and naked before You, requiring grace and imploring Your mercy. Refresh the hungry supplicant, kindle my coldness with the fire of Your love, illuminate my blindness with the brightness of Your presence. Turn all earthly things into bitterness for me, all grievous and contrary things into patience, all things worthless and created into contempt and oblivion. I lift up my heart to You in Heaven. Do not leave me to wander over the earth. Be sweet to me forever from this day forward, because You alone are my meat and drink, my love and joy, my sweetness and my whole good.

3. Oh If only You would kindle, consume, and transform me into Yourself! If only I could be made one spirit with You, by the grace of inward union, and the melting of earnest love! **Do not let me go away from You hungry and dry.** Rather, deal mercifully with me, as You often have dealt wondrously with Your Saints. What a marvel it would be if I could be wholly kindled from You, and utterly fail in myself, since You are a fire always burning and never failing, love purifying the heart and enlightening my understanding.

17

THE FERVENT LOVE AND VEHEMENT DESIRE OF RECEIVING CHRIST

Chapter Focus: Have you ever tried to recreate a joyous moment? It's difficult. Part of the joy of those moments comes from the surprising elements that arise to create the incidents of perfection: The weather, the location, the time of day, who was there, and our own predisposed attitude add up to that unique moment in time. There are no ordinary moments. When we are open to joy and happiness and love at all times, we see those incidents more frequently. Yes, we are prepared for such moments at weddings, graduations, sports playoffs, or upon the completion of a long-struggled for project (like writing a book!). And those are laudable. But when we ask for God to step into our ordinary moments, then there are no ordinary moments.

In asking to receive Jesus with a fervent desire, we easily make room for Him, perhaps in our stomach by fasting, or in our mind through Scripture study. I like to memorize Scripture because then I am oriented toward seeing its fulfillment in my daily walk at work or home. When I look forward to receiving Holy Communion on Sunday (or other days of the week), I make sure to prepare myself: my body, my mind, my soul. I am intentional and prayerful. Regardless of whether I receive some spiritual consolation or not, I know my prayer is heard as I approach the altar and receive the Host, regardless of whether I find myself worthy.

Thomas takes us to the Altar of God, and, approaching that Holy Place, reminds us that we can never be worthy. But Thomas advises us to desire to be worthy. He tells us to imagine being the holiest of saints in our desire to love, worship and receive the Body, Blood, Soul and Divinity of Jesus Christ. The Bridegroom calls and we answer. We approach, we leap for joy, like St. John the Baptist; or, like King David, we only need to be near Him to begin our dance of thanksgiving. Mindful of our many sins, we ask for mercy and forgiveness as we approach and receive. We open our mind and heart and will to Him, just as Mary did in her <u>fiat</u> (Lk 1:38): "Be it done unto me, according to Your Word."

CHAPTER 17, In Short.

1. I long to receive You, O Lord, with as much fervor as Your most holy Saint.

2. Though unworthy, I offer You the full affection of my heart as if I were worthy.

3. St. John the Baptist recognized You while in the womb of his mother, and at the sound of Your Voice: May I be like him.

4. Receive my prayers, O Lord my God, and my desire to praise You infinitely.

5. Let all peoples, nations, and tongues praise You and let Your Saints promise to remember me, for I am poor and needy.

SCRIPTURE MEMORY PRAYER: "Behold, I am the handmaid of the Lord; be it done unto me according to Your Word." (Luke 1:38).

Question: How would you have Jesus pray for you?

Key Quote: With the deepest devotion and fervent love, with all affection and fervor of heart, I long to receive You, O Lord.

~

The Fervent Love and Vehement Desire Of Receiving Christ.

The Disciple: With the deepest devotion and fervent love, with all affection and fervor of heart, I long to receive You, O Lord, even as many Saints and devout persons have desired You in communicating, who were altogether pleasing to You by their example of sanctity of life: They dwelt in all ardent devotion. O my God, Eternal Love, my whole Good, You are Happiness without measure, I long to receive You with the most vehement desire and appropriate reverence which any Saint ever had or could have.

2. Although I am unworthy to have all those feelings of devotion, still, I offer You the full affection of my heart, as though I alone had all those most grateful inflamed desires. Yes, also, whatever things a pious mind is able to conceive and long for, I offer and present to You with the deepest veneration and inward fervor. I desire to reserve nothing to myself, but freely and entirely offer myself and all that I have to You for a sacrifice.

O Lord my God, my Creator and Redeemer! with such affection, reverence, praise, and honor, with such gratitude, worthiness, and love; with such faith, hope, and purity I desire to receive You this day. I desire to receive You just as Your most Blessed Mother, the glorious Virgin Mary, received and desired You, when she humbly and devoutly answered the Angel who brought unto her the glad tidings of the mystery of the Incarnation. "Behold the handmaid of the Lord; be it unto me according to Your Word." (Lk 1:38).

3. And as Your blessed forerunner, John the Baptist, that most excellent of Saints, being full of joy in Your presence, leapt for joy in the Holy Spirit even while he was still in the womb of his mother. And after-wards, discerning Jesus walking amongst us, entirely humbled himself, and said, with devout affection, "The friend of the

Bridegroom, who stands and hears Him, rejoices greatly because of the Bridegroom's voice." (Jn 3:29). Even so I wish to be inflamed with great and holy desires and to present myself to You with my whole heart. And on behalf of myself and of all commended to me in prayer, I offer and present to You the jubilation of all devout hearts, their ardent affections, their mental ecstasies, and supernatural illuminations and Heavenly visions, with all the virtues and praises now celebrated and yet to be celebrated by every creature in Heaven and upon the earth. May You be worthily praised and glorified forever by all to the end of time.

4. Receive my prayers, O Lord my God, and my desires of giving You infinite praise and unbounded benediction, which, according to the multitude of Your unspeakable greatness are most justly due to You. These I give You, and desire to give every day and every moment. I call upon all celestial spirits and all Your faithful people to join with me in rendering You thanks and praises with pleadings and affectionate desires.

5. Let all peoples, nations, and tongues praise You, and magnify Your holy and sweet-sounding Name, with highest jubilations and ardent devotion (Ps 67;4-6). Let all who reverently and devoutly celebrate Your most high Sacrament and receive it with full assurance of faith be accounted worthy to find grace and mercy with You and intercede with all supplication for me a sinner. When Your people attain their wished-for devotion and joyous union with You and depart from You full of comfort, wondrously refreshed from Your holy, Heavenly table, let them promise to remember me, for I am poor and needy (Ps 40:18).

18

REFRAIN FROM CURIOUS
SEARCHING OF THE SACRAMENT,
BUT PURSUE BEING A HUMBLE
IMITATOR OF CHRIST, SUBMITTING
YOUR SENSES TO HOLY FAITH

Chapter Focus: I stood up in the class, trying to sound eloquent and prepared. I had read the case about interpreting the language of a contract against the person who wrote it and in favor of the person for whom it was written, but I wasn't stating the analysis very clearly. "I think the court erred because the Landlord didn't tell the Tenant about the Tenant's obligation to pay the rent by the 15th of the month," I said.

Professor Rudolph DeSeif shook his head in exasperation and pushed hard against the podium. "Sit down, Mr. Moore; you're no Karl Llewellyn. Did you even read the case?" And then to the whole class: "Did any of you read the case? Did you read the rental contract as the court quotes it?" He was clearly amazed by our mushy brains' inability to understand the text in front of us.

"It's easy," he said, "the court is telling you to always look at the plain meaning of the words in the contract. Now, Mr. Moore. Stand up again: Riddle me this: What do the words say? Are the words clear? Who wrote the words?"

I babbled something about Karl Llewellyn and DeSeif pushed his index finger into the casebook so hard that I thought the podium was going to collapse.

"Karl has nothing to say about this issue. He believed that what judges and lawyers actually do about the clash between a landlord and tenant is what the law is. And why are you reading him? You should just look at the text of the case. Look at the rental agreement. Look at the statute. What's it say, Mr. Moore? Please, save us all some time and try not to be an expert on the late, great, Professor Karl Llewellyn. Be an expert on what the contract says, as Karl would. In contract law, you always interpret the words against the person who wrote those very same words. The language is always construed to be in favor of the person for whom the words are written. Quit reading conspiracies and inaccuracies into the plain language of the text."

A light went on: This now made sense to me, even though in law school it seemed the cases and statutes we studied, and the methods used to interpret them attempted to hide the answers from us. In some classes, like First Year Contract Law, as a student I was always on guard for tricks and hidden meanings. I'd read commentaries on the commentaries, looking for clarity in a pool of murkiness. Sometimes, going down this path cost me time and mental anguish. I wouldn't accept the obvious answers even when the answers were printed right there on the page.

Sometimes it's that way in the mysteries of the faith. It can be difficult to set aside our curiosity regarding Jesus' claims considering His Body and Blood as offered at the Last Supper, and now re-presented during Mass.

Is it **REALLY** the Body, Blood, Soul and Divinity of our Lord Jesus Christ? The Church says so. More importantly, Jesus Christ says so. In Chapter 6 of St. John's Gospel, Jesus sets forth the plain meaning that we need to eat His Body and Drink His Blood to have Everlasting Life (Jn 6:22 and following). He insists on this even to the point of losing His Disciples (Jn 6:66-69).

Jesus further states this reality in the other three Gospels as recounted the Last Supper statements by our Lord, like this one in St. Luke's Gospel: "'Take and Eat: This is My Body.'" Then He took a cup, gave thanks, and gave it to them, saying, 'Drink from it, all of you, for this is My Blood of the Covenant, which will be shed on behalf of many for the forgiveness of sins (Matt 26:26-28; Mk 14: 22-24; Lk 22:19-20).'"

In law school, we practiced the Socratic method, where you answer one question with another question; and then another question. Jesus uses this method frequently in the Gospels, but not when talking about His Body and Blood and Everlasting Life. So my question for you is this: Will you believe the words of Christ Himself? If not, why not? What do the words say? Is it clear? Who said the words?

Like a good law student, you must read the words strictly against the One uttering the words, and in favor of those to whom the words are spoken. You get the picture. I've listened to other interpretations and heard the pretzel logic of some trying to slip out of the obvious words of Jesus. I'm with Prof. DeSeif on this one.

But of course, that's when our curiosity kicks in, doesn't it? Like the serpent in the Garden of Eden we hear "Did God really say, 'You shall not eat from any of the trees in the garden'?" (Gen 3:1) We start quibbling over the words, over the Sacrament, over the context. Thomas recommends that we take it on faith that Jesus meant what He said. We should always try to further our understanding of this great gift, but we should do so with an intention to appreciate the Gift that much more.

It is okay to submit to God's statement. I give you permission. It is also okay to say: "Lord, I believe, help my unbelief," (Mk 9:24) or "O God, be merciful to me, a sinner." (Lk 18:13). I applaud your humility. In this humble approach to the Sacrament, you can follow the simple steps God has laid out to receive Him and His Grace, rejecting our doubt as a temptation just as vile as any physical temptation. When doubt does sneaks in (and it will), look to the history of the Saints and their teachings.

God has revealed Himself to us in the breaking of the Bread (Lk 24:35). This is a two thousand year old mystery, not easily comprehended by human reason. Enjoy the mystery, its sacred nature.

Trust in Him. Believe Him. It's obvious and He means what He says.

~

CHAPTER 18, In Short.

1. God is able to do more than you can understand: an unhealthy searching into the Sacrament may cause you to sink into doubt.

2. Blessed is the simplicity which leaves behind the difficult paths of questioning and follows the plain and firm steps of God's commandments.

3. The enemy tempts you concerning faith and the Sacrament.

4. Go forward with a simple and sure faith, and draw close to the Sacrament with reverence.

5. All reason and natural investigation ought to follow faith.

~

SCRIPTURE MEMORY PRAYER: "Lead me in the path of Your Commandments, for that is my delight." (Psalm 119:35).

Question: Will you believe the words of Christ Himself?

Key Quote: Human reason is weak and may be deceived - but true faith cannot be deceived.

~

THE TEXT OF CHAPTER 18:

Refrain from Curious Searching of the Sacrament, but Pursue Being a Humble Imitator of Christ, Submitting Your Senses to Holy Faith.

The Voice of the Beloved: You must be cautious with the curious and useless searching into this most profound Sacrament so you will not be plunged into the depth of doubt. "Whoever is a searcher of Majesty shall be overwhelmed by its glory." (Prov 25:27). God is able to do more than you can understand. A pious and humble search after truth is allowed: it is always ready to be taught and studies to walk in the sound doctrine of the Fathers.

2. Blessed is the simplicity which leaves behind the difficult paths of questioning and follows the plain and firm steps of God's commandments (Ps 119:35). Many have lost their devotion while they sought to search into deeper things. Faith is required of you and a sincere life, not loftiness of intellect; not a deepness in the mysteries of God. If you neither understand nor comprehend the things which are beneath you, how will you comprehend those which are above you? Submit yourself to God, and humble your senses to faith, and the light of knowledge shall be given you, and these shall be profitable and necessary to you.

3. Some people are seriously tempted concerning faith and the Sacrament. But this is not to be attributed to themselves but rather to the enemy. Disregard your care for this. Don't dispute with your own thoughts nor answer the doubts which are cast toward you by the devil. Rather, believe the words of God, believe His Saints and Prophets and the wicked enemy shall flee from you. Often it will profit you much when the servant of God endures such things. For the enemy does not tempt unbelievers and sinners: He already has secure possession of them. But he tempts and harasses the faithful and devout by various means.

4. Therefore, go forward with a simple and sure faith, and draw close to the Sacrament with supplicating reverence. And whatever you cannot understand, you should commit to Almighty God without anxiety. God does not deceive you. You are only deceived when you believe too much in yourself. God walks with the simple, reveals Himself to the humble, gives understanding to children, opens the senses to pure minds, and hides grace from the curious and proud. **Human reason is weak and may be deceived - but true faith cannot be deceived.**

5. All reason and natural investigation ought to follow faith, and not precede it, nor break it. For faith and love do take the highest place, especially here, and work in hidden ways in this most holy and exceedingly profound Sacrament. God, Who is eternal and incom-

prehensible and of infinite power, does great and inscrutable things in Heaven and on earth, and His wonderful works are beyond discovery. If the works of God were of such sort that they might easily be comprehended by human reason, they should no longer be called wonderful or unspeakable.

KEY QUOTES, QUESTIONS, AND
SCRIPTURE MEMORY PRAYERS

1. **Scripture Memory Prayer:** "Come to Me, all you that labor and are burdened, and I will refresh you." (Matthew 11:28).

Questions: How can I bring God into my body when I can hardly spend one half-hour in devotion? What would happen if I would even spend one half-hour in devotion?

Key Quote: And behold, I have You here present on the Altar, my God, the Saint of saints, the Creator of all, and the Lord of Angels.

2. **Scripture Memory Prayer:** "Christ Jesus came into the world to save sinners. Of these, I am the foremost." (1 Timothy 1:15).

Question: Have you let the King feed you?

Key Quote: The charity of Christ never grows less, and the greatness of His sacrifice is never exhausted.

3. **Scripture Memory Prayer:** "Gladden the soul of your servant; to you, O Lord, I lift up my soul." (Psalm 86:4).

Question: Can you make the effort to receive Holy Communion at least one additional time this week? What would it take to do this?

Key Quote: Without You I cannot be, and without Your visitation I have no power to live.

4. **Scripture Memory Prayer:** "Taste and see that the Lord is good; blessed is the stalwart one who takes refuge in Him." (Psalm 34:9).

Question: What gifts has God given to you when you receive Holy Communion?

Key Quote: Illuminate, also, my eyes to behold this great mystery, and strengthen me that I may believe it with undying faith.

5. **Scripture Memory Prayer:** "[O]ur citizenship is in Heaven, and from it we also await a Savior, the Lord Jesus Christ." (Philippians 3:20).

Question: Are you praying for your Priests, Pastors, Deacons, Ministers?

Key Quote: God is the principal Author and invisible Worker, to Whom all that He wills is subject, and all He commands are obedient.

6. **Scripture Memory Prayer:** "Therefore whoever eats the bread or drinks the cup of the Lord unworthily will have to answer for the Body and Blood of the Lord." (1 Corinthians 11:27).

Question: How do you balance your unworthy nature against God's promise of Mercy?

Key Key Quote: [I]t is worth-while to know how I ought to prepare my heart devoutly and reverently for You.

7. **Scripture Memory Prayer:** "None of the crimes [you have] committed shall be remembered against [you; you] shall live because of the justice [God] has shown." (Ezekiel 18:22.)

Question: Which of the "So's" cause you the greatest discomfort?

Key Quote: For there is no oblation worthier, no satisfaction greater for the destroying of sin, than that you offer yourself to God purely and entirely with the oblation of the Body and Blood of Christ in Holy Communion.

8. **Scripture Memory Prayer:** "[E]very one of you who does not renounce all your possessions cannot be My Disciple." (Luke 14:33).

Question: Have you offered yourself to Jesus with all your heart?

Key Quote: Whatever you give except yourself is meaningless to Me; for I do not seek your gift, but you.

9. **Scripture Memory Prayer:** "For all in Heaven and on earth is Yours; Yours, Lord, is kingship; You are exalted as Head over all." (I Chronicles 29:11).

Question: How deep is God's Mercy? Are you letting Him apply His rich Mercy to your shortcomings and sins?

Key Quote: Behold, I commit myself to Your mercy, I resign myself to Your hands.

10. **Scripture Memory Prayer:** "Whoever loves Me will keep My word, and My Father will love him, and We will come to him and make Our dwelling with him." (John 14:23).

Question: How does it help you to put off the confession of your sins for a long time, or to defer Holy Communion?

Key Quote: Do not neglect Holy Communion because of some little vexation or trouble, but rather confess it, and forgive freely all offenses committed against you.

11. **Scripture Memory Prayer:** "[B]lessed is the one who takes no offense at Me." (Luke 7:23).

Question: What is the light of your soul - your Bread of Life?

Key Quote: For the Word of God is the light of my soul, and Your Sacrament the Bread of Life.

12. **Scripture Memory Prayer:** "I came that you might have life, and have it more abundantly." (John 10:10).

Question: Will you follow our Lord's command to come and receive? Will you answer His request (His plea!) to enter into your house?

Key Quote: Come and receive Me.

13. Scripture Memory Prayer: "My Beloved is radiant and ruddy; outstanding among thousands." (Song of Songs 5:10).

Question: Do I acknowledge Christ's Presence in the Blessed Sacrament regularly and with prayerful humility?

Key Quote: You are truly a God that hides Yourself, and Your counsel is not with the wicked, but Your Word is with the humble and the simple.

14. Scripture Memory Prayer: "As the deer longs for streams of water, so my soul longs for You, O God." (Psalm 42:2).

Question: On a scale from 1 to 10, with 1 being indifferent, and 10 being ardent, how would you describe your level of desire when receiving Holy Communion?

Key Quote: Oh, the impressive ardent faith of these people; they demonstrate the very proof of Your Sacred Presence!

15. Scripture Memory Prayer: "Then you shall see and be radiant, your heart shall throb and overflow." (Isaiah 60:5).

Question: How are you seeking the grace of devotion?

Key Quote: Where the Lord finds empty vessels, there He gives His blessing.

16. Scripture Memory Prayer: "I raise my eyes toward the mountains." (Psalm 121:1).

Question: What necessities do you need to lay open to Christ?

Key Quote: Do not let me go away from You hungry and dry.

17. Scripture Memory Prayer: "Behold, I am the handmaid of the Lord; be it done unto me according to Your Word." (Luke 1:38).

Question: How would you have Jesus pray for you?

Key Quote: With the deepest devotion and fervent love, with all affection and fervor of heart, I long to receive You, O Lord.

18. Scripture Memory Prayer: "Lead me in the path of Your Commandments, for that is my delight." (Psalm 119:35).

Question: Will you believe the words of Christ Himself?

Key Quote: Human reason is weak and may be deceived - but true faith cannot be deceived.

LETTER FROM THOMAS A'KEMPIS
TO ADRIAAN BOEYENS

Letter from Thomas Hemmerken of Kempen, Sub-prior of Mount St. Agnes of Zwolle.
To Adriaan Boeyens van Utrech. On the eve of the celebration of your twelfth birthday, that is, March 1, 1471, the Feast of Saint Siviard.

My Dear Adriaan.

On the night before your birthday, I hearken back to our conversation last spring, on the third day after the Feast of St. Servatius. Do you remember? Bishop Rudolf came to celebrate the installation of Otto Graes of Deventer, and Rudolph, son of Gerard, a native of Amersfoort as Clerks. Also installed was Henry Kalker, a Novice and Convert, who came from the region of Kleef. You probably remember him best, since he lived here before his investiture. As our unofficial tailor, he sewed up the tunic that you ripped when one of the carts caught your sleeve during your unloading of the fish barrels. You and your father (may he rest in peace) brought a generous supply of fresh fish for the feast along with casks of dried cod to help us feed the pilgrims and the poor, He helped us replenish our stores depleted by the long winter.

You'll remember that one of our novices who was scheduled to serve became ill, you stepped into his role at Holy Mass. Your Latin supplemental prayer was exceptional. Though your role was small, you treated it seriously as if you were the Bishop Himself! Such reverence and humility are rarities even among mature Christians. You and your father stayed with us for the worldlings' celebration which is when your father inquired about our Latin School here in Zwolle.

He was a fine man, your father. As a carpenter and boat-wright, he looked to St. Joseph as a model for Christian behavior. He was very proud of you and assigned you great responsibility for one so young. He told me, "Adriaan is always trying to figure out better ways of doing things. He's smart. He can read and write: always looking for books to borrow, no matter the subject. Takes after his mother, Gertrude."

I do not know if I told you that my mother was also named Gertrude. I miss her and my father every day. I treasure her silver feather bookmark, which my father made for her in his trade as a smithy. Like you, I learned his craft and happily assisted him whenever I could.

Now: As you return to our Latin School, my hope is that once you come of age you will join us as a novice. Being twelve, you are beginning to look around to decide what God wants you to do with your life: Marriage and a family, or perhaps, as I have heard, you'll take up your father's trade as a ship-right carpenter and fish carter. You certainly have talent, smarts and the physique to become an excellent boat-wright or whatever else you may put your mind to, suitable to your station in life and within God's will. Yes, I find that when we operate within God's will we accomplish the most. So what is God's will for you, Adriaan? What has He chosen you to do? What is His plan for you? Do you hear Him calling? How will you answer Him?

God calls each of us to a holy mission. That mission may be to your family. But for some of us that mission is to spread the Gospel across the village, country and even to foreign lands. To others, that mission reaches no further than outside our kitchen window to our children playing in the garden. God's gift to us is the ability to accept

His calling to do what He designed us to do as His agent in this world. For me, it took some time to realize my calling to take vows as a priest here in Zwolle. He called me here when I was about your age.

Many people prayed for me. My father, Johann wanted me to take over his trade as a silver smith. So he prayed for me to take on that vocation. After all, my mother already had her prayers answered since one of her sons became a priest. I may have told you about my brother, Jan. He was the first Prior at Mt. St. Agnes. As Jan's younger (and only) brother, I looked up to him as an example of holiness and dedication that he displayed as an Augustinian. He actually knew our Founder, Gerard Groote!

Meanwhile, I resigned myself to an apprenticeship as a silver smith. But then Jan persuaded father to allow me to attend the Latin School in Deventer; the very same Latin school you attend now in Zwolle. I was confused between my loyalties and interests: I kept going back and forth between taking over my father's shop and pursuing the books and writing I loved so much. With Jan's encouragement, my parents gave me their blessing to pursue becoming a novice. I was 18, a little late, I know, but my father needed help training up another apprentice to take my place. So I filled in wherever father's work demands required assistance until his new lad became a journeyman.

I still enjoy working with silver on occasion. During Christmas, you can see the large creche display at Mt. St. Agnes chapel, note that the halo of the Christ Child is a bit off-center: Some of my early work. In my later years, I enjoyed helping our local smith Philip Silver, pour chalices for our newly vested priests. I also helped him with the Bishop's Crucifix. So the next time you see our lord Bishop, you will have something to talk about.

I want to turn to the process you may encounter in deciding whether or not to pursue a life in service to God. No doubt you've heard the rumors about me: My brother Jan said I was the slow one of the family. "What's taking you so long, Thomas? What are you afraid of?"

You see, I kept delaying taking my final vows. That's what

happens when you struggle with your calling. I couldn't decide between becoming a journeyman or an Augustinian priest in the Modern Devotion; between becoming a husband and father or a celebrate Brother devoted to the Lord's work. The bold fact was that I met a certain girl named Regina. I'm convinced to this day that God put her into my life to confirm my vocation. By encountering such loveliness and holiness in her, I was able to set aside that part of my life for Him.

Our romance lasted for some time. Whenever I would travel home, Regina was waiting for me; our romance would rekindle. While I was in Zwolle, we'd write letters - always chaste, mind you - but with imaginings and longings and designs on our time together - and talk of raising a family, working in father's shop, sharing our lives. Kempen was a good place to live and work.

It was during one of those visits home when we were seriously discussing marriage - that Regina made fun of my freshly shaved tonsure. I had made her a gift of a silver prayer bracelet: not my best work, but fitting as a gift for a friend. Regina blushed at the gift. Well, I had made it too small for her: it would not go on over either of her hands. She laughed her gentle laugh, handing the bracelet back to me and said. "It's too small for my wrist and too big for my finger, Thomas." She then told me "While I love you, I think you would make a better priest than a silver smith."

Even though Regina said this in passing, her verbalized thought escaped her mind and entered mine, I couldn't help but think on it more and more. So here I was, trying to decide whether to become a journeyman smithy with a ready-made trade, ready made marriage to the beautiful Regina, or take my final vows.

By the bye, I later fixed the band through a clever trick my father showed me, opening the band by breaking the circle so the bracelet could expand.

Back to when I was twelve: Like you, I had come to Latin School at Deventer. I knew many fine brothers there, especially Prior Radewyns, who had written me a letter, much like this one. I dismissed it as the duty of the Prior to invite all young men to the priesthood.

I have kept that letter, along with the story it tells. So when Regina made mention that I would make a good priest, I went home that night and dug out Radewyn's letter.

You can read what the Prior said at the end of my letter to you, below.

Adriaan, I'll come to the point. My prayer for you is that you also become a priest. Accordingly, I want you to investigate the Brethren, to see if God may be calling you to share in our community. As you know, we are Augustinian monks, but serve our order within various monasteries, including the community surrounding Mount St. Agnes, but also houses all across Utrecht. We have chosen to adopt the rules laid out by Gerard Groote, the Founder of the Modern Devotion. As such, our charism goes beyond the general tenets of Augustinian life. We are priests and brothers and laymen and consecrated women who serve God at His Altar as well as serving His People in the community. We spread His Word through copying Holy Scripture, or by writing down important stories about holy people, like Prior Radewyns. We feed the hungry, provide shelter for pilgrims and those in need, and preach God's word to the common people in their own language - or provide them books to explain certain aspects of the Faith.

For example, accompanying this letter is a little book I put together for you. Its theme discusses many aspects of Holy Communion - also called the Eucharist - a word meaning "Thanksgiving". I won't expound upon the book's details here, since that is why I wrote the book. You are an intelligent lad, so I trust you will find a greater intimacy with our Lord by reading and meditating on the precepts of His true presence in the Eucharist.

One of the benefits of being a Priest is that you have the privilege of receiving Holy Communion every day. Through the Modern Devotion, we have been celebrating Holy Mass more often, and even distribute the Blessed Sacrament to the people at each celebration.

When I was your age, only the Priest received, unless it was Christmas or Easter, which is when the congregation received.

I wrote this book about Holy Communion over many years. Each chapter is either about a particular experience I had myself, or which was related to me by a Brother or a Sister in the Modern Devotion. Like other devotionals, I tried to make the chapter's subject a conversation. Either our Blessed Lord is speaking, or a Disciple is speaking - usually asking our Lord a question or responding to a topic initiated by our Lord.

For example: Christ tells us to approach Him boldly. We are to reply humbly, bringing our tattered, sinful nature to Him for refreshment. So while we can be bold, we can also humbly recognize God's great goodness to us in making Himself available to us as food. As such, we should Communicate as often as we are able (and are prepared), just like we need nourishment for our bodies every day. But that does not mean that we should treat the Sacrament lightly, or take it for granted. I think this is one reason Mother Church restricted reception of Holy Communion among the common folk in the past. We still must receive Holy Communion with an attitude of devotion - treating each reception as if this were our first, last, or only opportunity to receive Christ's precious Body and Blood.

As a priest I offer Holy Mass daily. Sometimes it is a struggle to stay focused on the miracle happening right on the Altar; right in my hands (although these are His Hands). So I pray to not be slothful or distracted or worse - indifferent. Indifference is the opposite of love. And love is at the heart of the Blessed Sacrament. So I pray for increased devotion before every Mass. Prior Radewyns taught me this ancient prayer:

> "Priest of God, celebrate this Holy Mass,
>> As if it were your first Mass;
>> As if it were your last Mass;
>> As if it were your only Mass."

I often have to be reminded that I am God's instrument - not worthy to be His minister. I act "in persona Christi" which you know is Latin for "In the person of Christ." I strive to be aware of this at every Mass, and approach to the Altar free of mortal sin. As a Priest, and as a penitent, I am blessed with ready access to Confession. I strive to serve at the Altar in a sinless state - a state of Grace. This is why I inserted some thoughts on Confession and repentance in this letter. I approach the Blessed Sacrament the same as if summoned to the King's Court. I wash up, don my best clothes, clean my sandals of manure; or even carry these to Court through the cow patch to avoid the stain and smell. We should do as much for our Lord. Because in examining our conscience and ridding ourselves of the stain of sin, we can make His home within us as clean as we would make our house if that same King decided to visit my little cell at Mt. St. Agnes. The Modern Devotion therefore offers daily Confession to the people for the same reason. You wouldn't want to have the King to your house if you decided to wait to clean it only once per year or once per lifetime! God wants us to be closer to Him, to be more like Him; to imitate Him. And for that, we need humility and purity; cleanliness and godliness.

I'm sure your academy studies tell you that the celebration of Mass is a re-presentation of our Lord's sacrifice on Calvary. Indeed, one in the same - traveling through time to Golgotha. God sees Jesus being lifted up for the forgiveness of our sins at the same time as the Host is elevated. It is then that we to join our sufferings with Christ and offer ourselves with Him - It is then that we take up our cross and follow Him. We consume His Flesh, becoming one with Him. Like Dismas, the Good Thief, we must die with Him but follow Him to Paradise, resting on His promise.

Therefore, do not waste suffering - neither His nor ours. Instead unite your sacrifice with Christ's to some purpose: to ease the pain of others, perhaps; or to succor the poor; to pray for the dead - and more.

Just like we do not take gifts, but instead receive gifts, neither do we take Holy Communion, we RECEIVE Holy Communion: Holy Communion is a gift. We share gifts. We give this holy gift as a prayer back to God to ask Him for some benefit for others or for ourselves. Adriaan, you may be too young to understand all of this talk of suffering, but I share this advice because I know you still mourn your father. Your time here has been fruitful, but I know you miss your home, your mother, your brothers and sisters. Suffering takes many forms. Lay it all at the feet of our Lord as a gift to Him, and receive His gift back to you.

For example, I like to offer my Communion for others. Today, before writing this letter, I offered my Communion for you. I can also offer God my sins, my works, the intentions of my friends and family. I can pray for those who have injured me, and forgive them. And of course, I always pray for the souls of my mother, Gertrude; my father, Johan; and my brother, Jan.

Bread of Life; Bread for Life, daily life and Eternal Life. He says: "Give us this day, our daily Bread...." This Holy Bread is for strength, growth, and protection. In order to defend ourselves and others against the snares of the evil one, we receive Holy Communion for the journey. And wouldn't you know it - anything and everything seems to get in the way of receiving the Blessed Sacrament; it's like the whole world conspires against us with its wickedness, obstacles, laziness, weather. And, of course, our own sin. We must push aside those obstacles, RUN to Confession, and return to the path of holiness. In short, do not neglect Holy Communion when it is made available to you; especially if you are thinking of becoming a Priest.

One thing more that can prepare you for a devout reception of God's Body and Blood: Holy Scripture. If you decide to join us here at Mt. St. Agnes, Scripture and its ink will be soaked into your mind, heart, and fingertips. Have you ever read about the prophet, Ezekiel? Ezekiel was told in a vision to eat God's Holy Word. And if you think about it, Jesus is the Word made into flesh like us. So when you receive His Blessed Body and Blood, you are also receiving His Holy Word. You are ingesting the Gospels!

The Blessed Sacrament is not some idle curiosity. Nor is it alchemy. I caution you not to experiment. Stay true to His path and follow it - without regret. So long as it is a Christian path, Heaven is yours. We take the elements of bread and wine, call the Holy Spirit upon these elements to become the Body and Blood of Christ and then distribute His bounty to His people, who say "Amen". It is a great mystery. Our Blessed Lord tells us in the Gospels that this bread and wine are His Body and Blood. There is no room for interpretation: There is only following Him, imitating Him, obeying Him.

Go forward then, with a simple and sure faith, and draw close to the Sacrament with reverence. Whatever you cannot understand, commit to Almighty God. God walks with the simple, as He did walking with Adam in the cool of the day. He reveals Himself to the humble as He did The Blessed Virgin Mary, gives understanding to children as He did with Samuel, opens Himself to pure minds as He did with St. Stephen, and hides grace from the curious and proud as He did with King Saul. He will not deceive you. It is when you believe yourself to the extent that your belief shifts from God to your own power and might, thinking of yourself to be like a god. That is when you are deceived: This is Adam's sin. Human reason is weak and easily deceived - whereas true faith cannot be deceived.

If the works of God were able to be easily comprehended by human reason, His works would no longer be called wonderful or unspeakable. You can use your natural reason and intelligence to follow this faith. Faith and love when placed first among your virtues, work in hidden ways, especially within this profound Sacrament. God Who is eternal, incomprehensible, and of infinite power, does great and inscrutable things in Heaven and on earth, and His wonderful works are beyond discovery.

As usual, my love for writing and "talking" has run on too long.

My final plea, Adriaan, is to read this book about Jesus' great gift to us. No - pray this book. Ask God what He would have you do. I look forward to discussing this with you on your return from Utrecht, or during your term break by letter.

Yours in Christ, Brother Thomas.

Post Script. Attached you will find my copy of the letter, which I referred to earlier, from Prior Florentius Radewyns.

Along with his letter is my gift for you upon your completing the Latin School. This is a story from that same Blessed Prior Radewyns, given to me during the time I was thinking about joining the priests and brothers here. Entitled "Three Pieces of Bread," it is a detailed account of a vision he wrote down regarding our Lord's last hours. He tells of his vision as through the pen of St. Luke and the eyes of St. Dismas, the Good Thief. Whether true or not, is a fine companion to the collection of meditations on the Eucharist.

**To: Thomas Hemmerken of Kempen, upon his matriculation from the Latin School at Deventer.
From: Father Prior Radewyns.**

On choosing to become a Priest of God.

My Dear Thomas: Your time here at the Latin School is quickly closing. Your classroom recitation last week was both creative and an inspiration. You demonstrated great mastery of your subject matter compared to your peers: of this your teacher and I were witnesses. Your Latin is flawless and elegant, almost lyrical. When I was your age, and mind you I was a good student, I knew the words and the declinations, but could not bring the language together to sound like poetry. And when you sang the Virgo Sacre and the Regina Coelli, I was moved. Your teacher said that you had rearranged the chant to make it more "smooth," whatever that means. Well done! As you know, I can barely whistle, let alone sing. But God gets to listen to me croak as He rejoices at your new baritone delivery.

I have prayed for you over these times, especially when your voice changed. I cried when you lost your angelic alto singing voice, but laughed with joy when I heard the deep resonance of your mature baritone emerge. "That's a voice of a preacher," I said to myself. "That's a voice that will get attention." Indeed, your new "manly" voice reminded me of Gerard Groote's. He had such a voice, bordering on the bass; it was commanding and inviting. Many came from miles around to hear him, including a pompous fop who thought he knew everything (me!). And so when I heard you declaim in class this week, as with your singing, I thought, "That is a young man!" I said to myself, "He's all grown up - no longer a boy. A young man who can speak, without fear, to an audience of speculatives, critics, and enemies is a young man that can speak on behalf of God."

I shared this observation with your brother, Jan.

Jan laughed and said, "Good luck with that one, Prior. Our Papa has big plans for Thomas - taking over the smithy business. And Mama says she already has her family priest - she wants grandchildren! And to top it off, he is pledged to a young woman. No doubt they will have many children!"

Far be it from me to dash the hopes of your parents, Thomas, but I must ask you to consider the priesthood: it is much like being a smithy.

As a smith, you work with a piece of silver: pinch and smooth, turn and bend, polish and file to achieve the finish you know lies within the metal, willing it into the shape that resides in your mind's eye. You treat iron different from copper, pewter different from silver. With iron, you sweep up the shavings and throw them into the dustbin or the fire. But not with your precious metals. Those you sluice through the separator, careful to rescue valuable dross. As a priest, you are much like a smithy. You stoke the fires of the Holy Spirit to fashion souls into His great design for each of us. Flaws are pounded and flattened by way of Confession and Penance - Fasting and Prayer, Alms Giving and Good Works. God grants you the power to solder together the brokenness that lies within every man and woman, fashioning them in God's image and likeness - achieving holiness by restoration and salvation. For He says 'Be holy, as I am holy.' Our Divine Lord gave us a model to follow, 'so that as I have done for you, you should also do.'

In this, we must imitate Christ. As Saint Paul tells us: we are to imitate him as he imitates Christ.

Thomas, I want to put into perspective the role of the priest. And I want to do so without diminishing the wonderful nature of working with your hands, raising a family, or contributing to the community. No doubt you could influence Kempen (or wherever you decided to settle) for the better. And no doubt, you'd be a pillar of the local Church.

Nevertheless, being a priest; a man of God, has eternal consequences on an order of magnitude that cannot be fully grasped. It's like the difference between looking through a normal pane of glass at a butterfly versus looking at that same butterfly through a magnifying glass where you can see the lines of demarcation between colors, or the tiny hairs on the antennae of the butterfly. God has a way of showing you His colors and details and plans. And then you get to communicate those insights with the people He puts in your flock.

Being a priest gives you the opportunity to talk about the immensity of God's compassion to everyone of your fellow creatures who share our earth-bound journey. God orders us to offer compassion to those to whom we minister: administering compassion and mercy are as unfathomable and limitless as the water in the sea or the sands of the dunes of Frisia. We do not do this under our own power, but through the power of Jesus Christ, when we act in His place.

You, in your youth, give me, in my old age, hope for the future; the future of the Modern Devotion, the Church, and its people. Through you and others like you, the Gospel must be spread and communicated across your own time and for the time to come. Whether Christ returns tomorrow or in one thousand years, the Gospel is commanded to be shared among all nations until Christ Himself tells us to stop. Our Modern Devotion does this through its ministers. We pass on this example to our flocks, to each other, and to our posterity. Some day, if you join us, you will pass on this invita-tion to others, and they will be your spiritual children - for eternity.

In our ministry, none of us belong to our parents: our community is our family. Just so, you are more than a child of your parents, but also a child of we teachers and ministers. While I pray for you to choose to live with us, together or apart our hearts and our prayers go with you each and every day. God has marked you while you have been here and commands us as a community to pray for you perpetually, regardless of your path.

One other thing: I am sharing a vision with you that I wrote wrote down after a dream I had the night before I decided to become a priest. I was older than you, and had encountered Groote during a street preaching of his. I have carried that dream around in my head for decades. And when I learned that you were looking to the trades instead of the priesthood, the Holy Ghost prompted me to write this vision/dream down for you. You may share it as you will.

THREE PIECES OF BREAD

A VISION AS RELAYED BY PRIOR FLORENTIUS RADEWYNS OF MT. ST. AGNES

The Good Friday Vision.

My vision began in preparation for Good Friday service. I was tasked to feed the cattle that hazy afternoon. I ventured into the barn to feed the oxen and, coming upon only one of the two, proceeded to the paddock to call in the other. I whistled. He looked over his shoulder at me, then turned his head back to the horizon, where I could see the rain clouds crawling across the plain. I whistled again, and called out to him, "Lucas! Come in and eat." The bull chewed his cud, disregarding my call. I moved toward him with the tether, wanting to end my chore before the storm soaked me. "Come along now, Lucas. What can be so entertaining about a storm on Good Friday?" I looped my tether through his nose ring and gently pulled him toward the barn. He was not having it and jerked back against my rope, throwing me in the air like straw. I landed against the paddock door and saw stars.

The next thing I knew, I was looking over the shoulder of a young Greek physician, much like a tutor over a student. I later discovered this student to be St. Luke, the Evangelist. He was not aware of my presence, other than to accommodate my view of his writing.

When I imagine my guardian angel, I see him looking over my shoulder in this way. He acts as a witness to all I see, do, hear, feel, write, smell, touch. Every emotion, thought, expression and statement is recorded, as if etched in wax, or even stone. And this is what I witnessed.

~

Luke's Chronicles to Theophilus.

My dear Theophilus, in my late winter letter, I promised to send you a complete account of events during my time in Jerusalem. As you know, my penchant for documenting oddities is only surpassed by my interest in history.

As fate would have it, I found myself in the employment of both the Jews and the Romans. Both wanted me for my skills as a physician. The Jewish Temple hired me to inspect their animals for purity and health while the Romans contracted with me to document prisoners' treatment before execution, that is, I make certain the prisoners are still alive before execution; certifying their deaths to validate bounties, estate settlements, and clearing the prosecutor's records.

The first part of what I am about to relate to you is an account of the testimony of a condemned man named Dismas, for which I will first present a brief background regarding his arrest. The second part documents Dismas' execution, including several complications not about Dismas, but surrounding the death of the Rabbi known as Joshua Bar Joseph of Nazareth.

I arrived at the Temple to inspect the sacrificial animals a few days before Passover. With the impending approach of the Jewish celebration, the crush of humanity in the city became tense as clashes among pilgrims brought about an increased presence of Roman soldiers. Much was made regarding the young Rabbi, Jesus or Joshua Bar Joseph or Jesus of Nazareth. Among the Greek speakers, like me, he is called Jesus of Nazareth since there are many Joshua's who are sons of Josephs. Jesus was rumored to be more than a prophet. He claimed to be from King David's lineage and House - claiming a kingship. This upset the Herodians, riled the Temple, and put the Romans on alert. It was at the Temple that the lives of Dismas and Jesus intersect.

~

A Few Days Before Passover.

Anyway, it was rumored that Jesus was coming to Jerusalem for Passover. So, like any curiosity seeker, I went out to see him. Of course, I had heard of Jesus, but I wanted to see the spectacle this man caused. Besides, it would serve as a good break from the boredom of inspecting sheep and goats. It had been only a few days since he entered Jerusalem, not on a grand war horse or stallion, but on a donkey! Thousands cheered him, proclaiming him King of the Jews, Son of David, Christos, Messiah. I heard them myself, "Hosanna! Hosanna in the Highest! Blessed is He Who comes in the Name of the Lord!" This display went on for some time. As I was near the entrance to the Temple when he arrived, I even saw him up close. I was to see him again soon more closely; intimately even.

You may recall that the mass inspection of sheep occurs outside, but the Temple priests insist on a final inspection when the worshiper goes in for the actual sacrifice. This generates another fee for them. I was hired to conduct those final inspections. I had finished inspecting a lamb for a worshiper's sacrifice just outside the entrance, when Jesus entered the Temple area. Jesus proceeded to drive out the money changers, merchants, hucksters, and charlatans, saying to them, "It is written, 'My house shall be a house of prayer, but you have made it a den of thieves!'" I remember him repeating this three times because the echo of the first faded into the marble as the third began.

In the Temple's space, the stone and marble amplify one's voice. A man with a well-trained tongue can pitch his voice and cause it to rumble throughout the Temple. Jesus' thunderous words shocked many, and his actions disturbed the chief priests, the scribes, etc. But what could they do? Even in the Rabbi's wrath, the worshipers hung on Jesus' words, turning their attention to him, and sharing in the disgust that had crept into the House of God. "They are prostituting the Temple!" called one. "Exploiters!" called another. When I attend worship with my mother, I see this corruption during the worship.

Regardless, and back to the chaos: Jesus wrapped a chord of ropes about his wrist and began to whip the coin boxes with great accuracy. He overturned tables. He kicked benches and upended pots and urns. His red face and piercing eyes gave evidence of his rage. It was the righteous indignation of a wild man, a warrior, or a king, distributing justice to those who know their guilt and acknowledge their punishment has come due.

As merchants scrambled out of harm's way, those buying goods dodged here or there to avoid the Rabbi and his chords. From my vantage point at the apex of the inspection booth that I first saw the two thieves, Dismas and Gesmas. Seeing an opportunity in the confusion, these two began to run about, shout, and bump into others, joining in as if they were the victims of the money changer's chicanery. But in the chaos, a purse disappeared into the folds of Dismas' tunic, or Gesmas, knocking the silver from the hands of a pilgrim, quickly caught it in his greasy palms. Even as Jesus and his followers drove the merchants from the area, Gesmas, and Dismas gathered a significant amount of silver.

As the Temple guards arrived on the scene to put down the riot, Jesus and his disciples left the building. The two thieves were collecting their last purses and coins when an unfortunate Temple guard accosted them. As Dismas turned from his latest victim, he ran headlong into the guard. The guard clubbed Dismas across his brachial nerve, and Dismas collapsed. Gesmas, who was behind the guard, rammed his head fully into the back of the guard, knocking the cudgel free. Gesmas, recovering the cudgel, brought the club's full weight and power down upon the guard's helmet, cracking his skull and killing the guard instantly. The remaining Temple guards, now aware of the skirmish, turned their attention to their comrade and fell upon the two thieves, taking vengeance upon them during their arrest. Gesmas blamed the groggy, reviving Dismas, but the witnesses pointed to Gesmas' murderous actions. The Temple leaders quickly plotted a tie between Jesus and the guard's murder, labeling the two thieves as Jesus' accomplices and disciples. They did this by heaping scorn and accusations on Dismas and Gesmas and then directing conspiratorial blame upon the actions of Jesus as the chief instigator. Because of their obvious guilt and abundance of witnesses, Gesmas and Dismas were quickly escorted through the Roman justice system, sentenced to death, and taken to the dungeon. They were sentenced to be crucified on Preparation Day.

~

Roman Justice.

Roman justice demands that those receiving a death sentence record some claim of innocence, regardless of whether those pleas of innocence will be ignored or listened to. They also insist on having a physician inspect each condemned man to ensure he serves out his sentence. On Thursday of that week, I was summoned to the dungeon to provide the prisoners with essential medical treatment, and ultimately, validation of death. Since I was already at the Temple, the Romans had me certify the death of the Temple guard and swear to what I saw at the Temple, writing an affidavit about my feeble attempt to revive the guard. It was then that the Romans, always looking to save a coin, "recruited" me to verify that the prisoners remained alive before execution. The Romans are very efficient. I had to take both perpetrators' statements, which you will read below: mostly the fantasies of dying men, as you shall see, but curious nonetheless.

A word on Roman torture, they are masters at its administration: A criminal sentenced to die may not be tortured to the point where the Empire would be denied its right to execute the man. Dismas and

Gesmas endured several physical trials, none of which were life-threatening: Dismas had his legs covered in molasses, whereupon stinging ants were released upon the molasses and allowed to ravage him. The stings were painful and caused puss-filled sores with unquenchable itching, but were not life threatening.

Dismas counted himself lucky, as normally he would have had either or both of his hands cut off to be hung around his neck - the penalty for thieves. This was denied his captors, however, because then some jailer would have to carry his crossbeam to crucifixion. A very inefficient use of labor.

His brother, Gesmas, blamed for the actual killing, was punished more severely. On the first day, his food scraps were laden with salt, yet he was given no water, which resulted in a maddening thirst. As sundown approached, the jailer affixed cage around Gesmas' head containing two scorpions. These nocturnal arachnids awoke to sting him several times, aiming mainly at the eyes, nose, and lips. While their venom is strong and their stingers relentless, the jailer had stunted their pincers so Gesmas would not lose his eyes in the process - again, not from any sense of humanity on the part of the Romans, but simply as a practicality of the eventual execution. No one wants to lead a blind man up a hill. Once morning came, vipers were released into Gesmas' clothing - a punishment for betrayers. These bit him mercilessly, but as they were young vipers with weak venom, lacked the power to kill him, only inflict pain. And thirst. Gesmas remained stoic throughout, not wanting to give his torturers any entertainment at his expense. "Nothing will change if I whine or cry out," he thought, "they'll only introduce some new menace."

∾

Confession of Dismas the Thief.

Below is a record of the testimony of the thief and murderer, Dismas. I went into the cell to hear from the three condemned. I first attempted to interview Gesmas, who would not speak to me, because he considered me to be an agent of the Romans. I next turned to Rabbi Jesus, who was unconscious. This left Dismas, of whom I asked a series of questions. As you can read for yourself, he was so confused that he would only discuss whether he had been fed or not. He was fixated on food. Here is our exchange.

I proceeded to ask him routine questions, such as:

Who is feeding you? Are you being fed? What about water? How are your wounds?

Dismas replied: "The jailer brought us three dark crusts of moldy bread, which he took from his filthy apron. He fished the morsels from the centurion's garbage pile. Usually, the best of the remains of their food orgies goes to the jail guards. From there, they pass the spoils to minor, well-connected offenders; ones not condemned to die. Once they eat, anything left comes to us. As the jailer says, 'why waste food on a dying man?'"

Gesmas guffawed at the question.

"In spite of all that, I was so hungry that every time the jailer' moved, I hoped he was sorting some crusts for us, a great incentive to behave. Malcontents don't get fed. Or they spike your food with salt. Ask Gesmas.

"I heard we are supposed to die Friday, but they might change their mind because of Passover. So they are feeding us sparingly, just in case we hold-over until Sunday. We Jews don't like such violence to interfere with our high holy days. Sometimes the Romans release a prisoner at Passover to curry favor with the Sanhedrin. Perhaps this year, it'll be me. I've been very cooperative. I gave them a lead on Bar Abbas.

~

Three Pieces of Bread.

"So HERE I AM, watching the jailer, waiting like a trained monkey to jump at a fig when the jailer appears. He stops, looks at the Rabbi - Jesus, who came a few hours ago, and says, 'Hey you! Your Royal

Highness – if you can catch this, it's yours.' He then tossed three bread crusts, one at each of us, like I'd throw bones to a dog. He launched the first one at the Rabbi: 'Enjoy that,' he said, 'it's your last supper. How nice that you've got your disciples here to celebrate with you!'

"Then he turned his attention to Gesmas and me: 'Hey, you two murdering thieves! 'I'll wager there'll be a great battle between you two; let's see how - if mamma taught you to share.' This should be good!' here's yours,' he said, tossing the other two bread crusts toward me and Gesmas.

"Gesmas is so sarcastic, he called out,'Be sure to send down a flask of your best wine as well. I'm thirsty."

"The jailer ignored the comment, tossing the bread to the area between Gesmas and me. I turned, following the arc of the crusts, and batted at them, jumping to catch one but was caught short by the collar and chains around my neck. I was jerked back to the floor and looked hungrily at the scraps that fell between us. I stretched out my leg to try and grasp the crust with my toes, but both pieces landed outside my reach but within the length and reach of Gesmas' chains. Gesmas looked at me like he did when we were kids, a smirk of duplicity on his face. He quickly stuck out his foot, covering both pieces of bread and pulled these within his reach.

"I begged, 'Come on, Gesmas, throw me one, will you? I'm starving!'

"'Not on your life,' he said. 'I won the bet, fair and square. You lose. Again. You always lose betting against me. You should know that by now, brother. If I am going to die today, why not go out on a full stomach? After all, like the jailer said, 'Why waste good food on a dying man?'"

"I was desperate in my hunger and cursed Gesmas. Three days without food is an eternity. You start to hallucinate, and hunger pains are no longer reminders but a constant ache, like when you get a cramp in your leg that doesn't go away.

"I pointed my finger at him, 'You are more despicable than I could ever have imagined. Even when we were boys, you were mean and rotten to me. You have always done this to me. Because we were brothers I befriended you. Mom said I had to look out for you. I felt sorry for you. I stayed with you even though you were evil and beyond hope, but I never figured that in your dying hours, your brutish nature would show itself to deny a crust - a moldy crust - to your own brother; your only friend."

The guards laughed and traded small talk as they prepared the cross beams, and Dismas continued, "I bet against the odds: I gambled that a dying man, especially a brother, would be repentant and seek mutual comfort during such a time, and if not for the sake of that friend, at least in some way to atone to God for his sins. I was wrong, of course.

Gesmas looked at me, amazed, 'Fool,' he said, 'My sins are my own. Leave them to me. There is no God as you and I know. Would God allow this dreaming Rabbi to die in such a way? No. There's no God. No mercy. No forgiveness. So why pretend? I won't pretend for you, for him, or anyone. I'm going to feed myself. You can starve. Your hunger will only last until you reach the top of Skull Hill. Then your hunger pains will be replaced by other pains, and you will forget your hunger. Again, you bet against me. Again, you lose.'

"He chewed down the first piece, 'If you had received the two pieces, I bet you would've kept them for yourself, and I would not have blamed you, only hated you more than I already do. If you would have shared one crust with me, I'd think you a soft fool. Yes, you soft Momma's boy. And it was always the other way around. I've always protected you, her favorite, just to get some sort of affection from her. "Take care of Dismas, Gesmas, he's not as tough as you," she'd say. "Don't let the others pick on him. You'll see, someday he will rescue you, pay you back." Well, today's a good day for a rescue. But I'm done with you, your schemes and dreams: Yes, you're a dreamer, like this Rabbi here.

'Ever since we were children calling out to one another to play games, you always pretended. I always protected you from the other kids who picked on you for being small and sly and smart. I admired you; I resented you too, every time you hid behind me. Later, when you were scoring a big deal, some scam. You'd say, "We'll be rich, Gesmas! Just help me on this one gig with Zacchaeus." Of course, that was another failure of yours. And I was fool enough to follow you. At least we got some excellent meals and.... Well, no one can feed or rescue us from here or even play a dirge for us because we'll get no funeral. I've been stung so many times I doubt I can even whistle. There's no dreaming here, the reality is: They'll strip us and hang us until the birds pick apart our bodies and then toss us into the potter's field. The only funeral dirge we get will be from the crows rejoicing at their feast of eyeballs. There's only one way out of here: death's trap door.'

Gesmas chewed through the bread and gulped.

'And Friend? I know we are brothers, but I don't have any friends, just marks, victims, fellow travelers, and co-conspirators. When did you ever think that I was your friend? Were we ever really friends? More like you tolerated me, and I tolerated you - used each other, really, based on empty promises to Mother. She thought we were a good team. But I don't think she wanted us to turn out as a couple of low-life grifters. Not exactly my aspiration either. I'm glad she didn't live to see us. And you did a great job lying to her on her death bed. "Momma, Gesmas and me are opening a shop outside Jerusalem's walls. We're going to sell souvenir trinkets to pilgrims and tourists." Well, we sort of did that with our gang of thugs and thieves, tricking the bumkins out of their silver and selling stolen cloaks and sandals to unsuspecting travelers. That worked pretty well until that merchant we rolled saw a tourist wearing his fancy cloak. But you had your wits and talked us out of it before we got into trouble, and I had my muscle, ready to fight any on-comers. We made a lot of coin. We lived for the day. But we always blew our gains on other schemes. 'Gesmas, the real money is in the Temple,' you'd say. 'We've got to get into those markets. Money changing. High prices for small animals and birds. Full purses for the priests.' I always respected you for the good thief and sly grifter you are, nothing more.

'So what did you expect, brother? Of friends, I have none. And neither do you. If you did, they'd be here with you, rescuing you or at least dropping some food through the grates. Or a skin of wine or water for me. I'm so thirsty.

'Yes, you're as pathetic as Prince Dreamer here,' he jerked his thumb toward Jesus. 'Abandoned by all his friends, betrayed by his cowardly strap hangers – sold out, as I heard. I'm just sorry we didn't get to him first. He'd have brought us some silver. Betrayed by his own. He couldn't even trust his own gang! I trust no one but the Romans. You always get what they promise: death, death on a cross.'"

"Gesmas laughed, turned to me, and said, 'In fact, now that I think of it, you're more pathetic than the Rabbi! You didn't even have anyone to betray you unless you count me.' Gesmas then chewed down the remaining crust.

"I couldn't look at him after that, so I turned my back to him, facing the dark corner. Gesmas was right. Would I have shared my crust with him if I had received both? I thought so in my fanciful view of myself, but perhaps that was the imagining of a desperate, condemned man. Would I have shared the crust with Rabbi Jesus? Truthfully, prophet or not, I'd have let him starve."

I then asked Dismas to tell me more about the Rabbi.

"Over the last three years, I always seemed to be on the fringe of the Rabbi's Jerusalem preaching. Of course, I was familiar with such tricksters, magicians, and charlatans. As Gesmas said, I used to form alliances with them to cheat their followers and divide the spoils. Their honeyed words deluded the people, especially the rich widows, shaking the silver from their palms with promises of hopes and dreams.

"Strange, this one seemed to appeal to the poor, so I waited for him to beg for their pennies, but the plea never came. I waited for him to scam them, and I thought I could pretend to become one of his followers to get in on the action, but as I got closer and talked with others on the fringes, I could not see through the scam, the cheat, the grift. How do you get money from feeding thousands of people? No collection was taken up!

"You look confused so I'll explain:

"I followed him to a field one day. Everyone ate bread and fish, and I thought, 'This is it! Today these goons will extort money from the people as they leave.' But that's not what happened. They gathered up leftovers and then gave the food to the poor. It was the craziest thing I had ever seen!

And then Zacchaeus and Gesmas and I decided to fleece these sheep by charging them a bridge toll tax and pocketing what's left. It's a scam, Zacchaeus and I used it a few times against pilgrims coming into the city. Works every time!

He rambled on: "Giving hope to the poor is its own pathetic delusion. Why would anyone whip up such a falsity? I mean, they are poor because of their sins or their father's sins, right? But this guy made everyone BUT the poor mad at him: the Jewish rulers hated him. You could feel the hate come off their glares and sneers like sparks on an anvil. Then they hammered out the most scandalous gossip, tossing it about like slag on a walking path.

'He's a drunk. He associates with prostitutes. He's friends with tax collectors. He's a blasphemer.' At first they only whispered, but soon these became shouts. My kind of guy, I thought.

But their jealousy went beyond mere words. It's how he ended up here with Gesmas and me.

Pilate's spies kept watch over him under suspicion as a rioter and all around political trouble maker. Yes, Pilate was under Rome's scrutiny. Rumor has it that one more mess up, and he's out for good.

Herod, well, Herod is jealous of him: If Herod came through the streets like Jesus did earlier this week, they wouldn't be throwing flowers at him and palms at his feet. It'd be dung for him and slingshot stones at his horses. He'd be the ass ridding the horse!

"I AM STILL PERPLEXED by the people, though. The common folk, the poor, the marginalized - His gift of hope to them does seem cruel in retrospect. But I think he meant it at the time, which seemed to elevate the Rabbi in the eyes of the fools that followed him. They wanted to make him their King, but only if he could feed them bread every day. Yes, this conjurer of tricks somehow fed thousands. But I never saw him get a silver shaving from the poor when affecting a cure. Under what cup is he hiding the ball? Where's the game?

If he were King, if he can do that again and again, why, he could end starvation throughout the land. Just think of it! Well, there were more rumors and more fantastic stories, especially during the high holy days. 'Jesus healed a man blind from birth. Jesus cast out demons into a herd of pigs. Jesus raised a little girl from the dead!

Then, when his friend died, Jesus raised him from the dead - after four days! I couldn't believe it.' The stories grew more fantastic with each fanatical fringe element that followed him. Besides, I can't imagine anyone wanting to be King of the rabble that followed him - ignorant peasants combined with the sick, lame, and lazy. He was worse, in a way, than Gesmas and me. At least we were open about our thievery and our intimidation. We weren't pretending to help anyone but ourselves. And everyone knew it.

"I mentioned Zacchaeus. During my association with him, I found out what this Jesus was really like. You see, in between heists and schemes, I had been living at Zacchaeus' house. I worked for him as his tax collector, acting as a servant and runner in his tax extortion enterprise. Gesmas too. Many times I'd help identify the tax cheats. Then we'd use whatever means necessary to gather the taxes. Gesmas liked that part.

"Some months ago, Zacchaeus had word that Jesus was coming through our village. His coming was good news! We made a plan with Zacchaeus to profit from the crowd of followers. Like the tax collections I mentioned, Zacchaeus, Gesmas, and I conspired to extort coins from Jesus' followers during his trek through the village: a toll right at the bridge. Zacchaeus would spy out the crowd and signal the heavy purses to Gesmas or me. The wealthier pilgrims would gladly pay the freight for the rest of the suckers: there was plenty for all. I would embezzle my cut, and Zacchaeus would still pay us a share of the final tolls collected. As foretold, Rabbi Jesus turned up at Zacchaeus' village. The crowd was following him like a bunch of sheep ready for shearing. Seeing us, they all dug at their purses to pay the toll.

"But then I saw Jesus meet with Zacchaeus, 'This is finally it,' I thought. 'something is up. I will finally find out his gimmick, the gig, or the trick. He's probably skimming.' And what do I care, so long as I get my share? But old Zacchaeus, if you know him, is a master extortionist, blackmailer, and fraudster, on top of being the most corrupt tax collector this side of Jericho. He sees all the angles. I thought that perhaps he'd scam the Rabbi - get a premium, then undercut him - that's Zacchaeus' style. Once I saw the two together, I knew there had to be something else going on, some complicated conspiracy to clip the sheep.

"But then Jesus invited himself to dinner with Zacchaeus, and everything changed. Zacchaeus became a disciple of Jesus that day. I couldn't believe it. I couldn't see the angles. He seemed genuine. The old tax collector returned all the toll money! You must understand Zacchaeus would rather part with his children than his money!

"Sure, we made off with our percentage of the silver, but I saw Zacchaeus return tax money to the pilgrims over and above what Gesmas and I had collected and skimmed. He dug into his treasure like he was pulling out a bad tooth. He gave away a fortune that day, and none of it went to Rabbi Jesus.

"Of course, I was alarmed by this sudden restoration of Zacchaeus' scruples: We feared retribution from Zacchaeus and his gang; you know from a change of heart when he sobered up. So instead of joining him for dinner, we slipped out to Jerusalem to get lost in the crowds of the big city with its Passover anonymity.

"Which brings us back to today. Our friend the jailer throws out three pieces of bread. As you heard, Gesmas got two, and the Rabbi got one. As the jailer walked off, I made eye contact with the Rabbi. He looked away from me, threw his shawl over his head, and turned to the corner, murmuring words as if praying. I expected him to eat in private and spare me from watching him eat: A small kindness, even in this place. But then he turned toward me, holding the bread crust in his open palm, lifting it up to Heaven. He closed his other hand over the bread and shut his eyes in Thanksgiving - blessing the bread. Through his broken lips, Jesus tossed the crust toward me and said, 'I have food to eat, which you do not know.' I didn't know what he was talking about. Many prisoner's family members bribe the jailers to obtain food, so at first I assumed he had worked something out with the jailers for some tastier morsels better than moldy bread. But in a moment, I realized this was his sacrifice for me.

"The crust landed squarely at my feet. I picked it up in wonder. What I had imagined I would do in my best moment, for my brother, he did in his worst moment, for a stranger. Even though I knew about him, he didn't know me from Adam. He owed me nothing. He wanted nothing in return.

"I picked up the bread. My stomach ached with hunger. I wanted to shove the whole crust in my mouth at once, but my chains and wounds made me take the bread apart.

"You will not believe this, but the stale, moldy crust changed. What had been a brown moldy crust was no longer grotesque with maggots and stale, weak gravy but was now fresh and spongy, made of the finest wheat.

"I tore off a piece and put it to my tongue. The sweetness of the morsel ran across my mouth, and I chewed with delight. The flavor did not fade as I swallowed a portion, taking time to make the sensation last. The dampness around me seemed to fade; even the iron manacles softened on my flesh. Sure, my cuts and bruises remained, but the throbbing dissipated. I swear. Not that you will believe me."

"Go on," I said.

"I remember looking at the crust when I tore off another piece and said to the Rabbi, "Thank you, Jesus. Will you have some?" And Jesus shook his head 'no' and smiled crookedly through his bruised lips. I continued to eat the bread and eat the bread and eat the bread. The bread I broke away to consume did not diminish the crust!

"After some time, finally sated, I turned to Gesmas. Gesmas had been distracted by his painful stings. Now swollen from the venom, the scorpion and asp stings began to itch with a fiery intensity. 'Would you like some bread, Gesmas? It is the best bread I have ever tasted. The Rabbi shared his with me.'"

"'Of course, it's the best you'll ever eat!' he growled, 'It's going to be

the last thing you ever eat. Yes, I'll gladly take some. Throw it over.'
Bread for the journey.'

"I threw the crust to him, and the piece landed next to his empty
water bowl. Picking up the piece, he laughed at me. "You're delu-
sional, Dismas. This moldy, stale crust is worse than the piece I stole
from you, although the maggots will provide a little meat to the
bread. I just crush 'em and spread the little worms across the bread
like butter. But I'm hungry." Gesmas then tore at the hard, moldy
crust and wolfed it down.

~

Thirsty Gesmas. A Visit to Sparky. A Crown for His Majesty.

"About then, the jailer opened the cell door. 'C'mon, your Majesty.
Time for the royal treatment. Old Sparky's waiting for you.'"

"'Sparky?' I asked.

"'Sparky is the iron-tipped, nine-tail whip. When it kisses you, you
know you've been kissed. What's fun about Sparky is that as you're
being whipped, the tips touch each other and create sparks! It's something to see! Sometimes, like now, we like to wait until dark to use it.
Quite a show!'

"Gesmas yelled out, 'Bring us water!' The jailer laughed in
mockery and disappeared. A few minutes later, he returned with a
pail, letting the Rabbi drink from the ladle. Was this compassion? I
don't know. He gently poured water over Jesus's back, and the water
ran down his arms. Fully sated, the Rabbi let the water run into his
palm and splashed his face. He did it again as I looked on, then
flicked the droplets at me while saying something difficult to make
out through his broken lips. I think he said, 'Receive your vindica-
tion,' or something like that. I think it was a psalm. Funny how that
stuff can come back to you. The jailer then passed the ladle to me
with a grunt. I noted that Jesus' blood tainted the water, but I was
thirsty and didn't care. Then the jailer unbuckled Jesus and led him

away. Gesmas called out again, 'Hey! Where's my water?' as the jailer carried the bucket away.

"I awoke sometime later as the cell door creaked open. It was still dark, but I could see Jesus stumble to his corner as the jailer again brought in the bucket. 'Here's your water, scum!' he said, pitching the water to the ground just outside the chain length of Gesmas. Gesmas bent forward, extending his arms, and barely dabbed his fingers in the nasty puddle to wet his lips, quietly cursing the jailer.

"Gesmas, seeing the Rabbi, chuckled quietly, shaking his head and saying,' Looks like he got a good licking from old Sparky. And a crown of shame.'

"I could make out the irons clasping shut over Jesus' ankle - the one place on his body that was not stripped, bruised, or beaten. There'd be no more crooked smiles today; his beard was matted with blood, spit, and dirt. I could only imagine the punishment he endured at the whipping post. The tattered horse blanket hung (or rather stuck) to his shoulders. In the dark, I wasn't sure if it was purple or just bled through; regardless, the blood had glued the fabric to the Rabbi's back and sides.

"Something else I could not quite make out in the dull light: something gripped Jesus' head like a Legionnaire's helmet. As the dawn penetrated the darkness of the jail cell, it looked as if he wore a wreath around his head, similar to a champion's wreath, something the Romans awarded to their athletic heroes, poets, and generals. But this one appeared to crawl around his forehead. As the light increased, I could see it was made of sticks and that the crawling movement was his blood, leaking from everywhere, running down his brow and temples into his beard.

"I felt sick to my stomach. My knees began knocking. I spread my arms to either wall for support: Dizziness set in as I wondered if I was Sparky's next guest. After all, Gesmas and I had killed a Temple guard. Not that the Romans cared about the Jewish guards, but it was an insult to Roman law and order.

"As if reading my thoughts, the jailer said, 'Don't worry, they only use Sparky for Caesar's enemies. You don't qualify. They had it all set up for Bar-Abbas, but, and I still can't believe it - the Governor let him go—some Jewish Holiday tradition.

"'Make no mistake, you two will still get crucified, along with this one. There'll be plenty of pain to go around. We're generous that way. You'll be laughing at the fear you have now over Sparky. Most guys pass out from the pain. But they save the humiliation of Sparky for pretenders like him. His Majesty was strangely silent through most of the lashes, though lots of mumbling.'"

"'What is that on his head?' I asked.

"'Thorns. A crown fit for a King of his sort. He now can rule over his kingdom of scorpions, spiders, and thieving killers like you two. I've got a few more for his friends if they show up.' A guy outside the city makes them for us for just such an occasion.

"I focused on the crown of thorns as Jesus faded into unconsciousness, his head falling against the wall, thorns snapping, piercing his ears and scalp."

～

My Vision-Dream Fades.

Thomas, as Jesus faded into unconsciousness, my vision-dream faded into the darkness of the dungeon at the same timeI saw the physician set down his pen. It was like having two dreams at once.

I tried to focus my eyes, tried to read the next words on his page, as one does in a dream, but to no avail. I lay stone still, searching my mind's eye for a door or window back into the vision, when I heard the jingle of keys and turn of a lock bolt. From the corner of my dream I caught the hem of the young physician's cloak rising up the stone steps. I reached for the robe, felt its texture and the tension of his motion pulling me along. The jailer's light appeared above the head of the three condemned as he directed them along to the wooden beams and chains on the cart.

～

The Journey to the Top of the Hill and What Happened There.

"'Time to go, boys! 'It's a short walk, but it's all uphill. Let's get this over with; I'm meeting a lady tonight, and the sooner I get you filth on that hill, the sooner I can hand you off to the execution detail, and then I'm done for the day.

"'I'm going to tell you what to do. If you disobey me, you'll get a beating worse than Sparky would dole out, and you'll still have to move. If we have to force you, me and the boys tie you naked, face down, between a couple of donkeys and we chase you up the hill. That's a real crowd-pleaser, but then I have to load your cross beams on a separate cart, which means more work for me. So, let's do it the easy way, and it'll go quickly for you - well, for the two of you murderers, anyway. This one, his Majesty, gets nothing but the best treatment. You may want to stay behind him a little if you know what I mean. The word is that Herod will have a group of his strap-hangers there to throw things at the Rabbi. Herod wants to see him perform a miracle.

The following hours were filled with a dusty, chaotic din of suffering. The April morning sun added to the torture. Flies bit and annoyed, bystanders threw rotten food, spiting wine and flinging stones at the cross-bearers. Man's cruelty was on full display. Typically no one watches these executions except the victims' families. But there was quite a crowd. I suspect many were paid to show up, and others were Rabbi Jesus' followers.

The soldiers beat Jesus mercilessly at every step. One cadre tore his tunic from his body, opening his whipping wounds again, while another dowsed him with salt water. The crowd was similarly cruel. Bystanders picked up and threw the worst refuse and animal dung at Jesus. One man tripped him as he struggled with his crossbeam, and his strength gave out as he splayed into the rocks and dirt two or three times. Jesus was so near death from the scourging that the Romans drafted a passer-by to assist him.

Still, a few acts of charity surfaced from the mob. A young woman came to his aid to wipe the filth from his face. He managed to speak to a small group of women who mourned him. His disciples were otherwise not in attendance and nowhere to be seen. Though the Romans were on alert, no rescue attempt materialized. Likewise, a pause interrupted the chaos as Jesus stopped to speak to another woman, who I later found out to be his mother. It was as if the whole world had stopped to listen to them; how she could hear his slurred and bloodied words amazed everyone. But then mothers can hear their children, no matter what, can't they?

Usually, these convicts are prodded and dragged screaming up the hill, or worse. I've seen the jailers give them the donkey treatment Dismas mentioned. This hanging is different. Despite all the vulgarity and noise, a certain dignity accompanies this crucifixion because of the Rabbi. On the way up the hill, as the crowd throws garbage and refuse at him, he turns and looks, not in challenge, but from the vantage point of a king or general surveying his kingdom. Of course, many are here in quiet support of the Rabbi: waiting in expectation of something extraordinary to happen: for him to break free or cast a spell changing the circumstances. The rest are either hirelings or the usual death-as-entertainment crowd.

It seems as if Jesus willingly undergoes the disgrace of the moment, but when he wants an encounter, as with his mother or the woman who wiped his face, the theater of petty derision ceases for the sacredness of the moment. Though in chains and burdened, he is in complete control - even in his weakness, suffering, and falling, he is somehow in control. He rises above the pain and anguish to focus on the particular person in front of him. For example, as I mentioned, he stopped and spoke to the town's women just now. I heard him say, "Do not weep for me but weep for yourselves and your children. For behold, the days are coming when they will say, 'Blessed are the barren, and the wombs that never bore, and the breasts that never nursed!' Then they will begin to say to the mountains, 'Fall on us,' and to the hills, 'Cover us.' For if they do this when the wood is green, what will happen when it is dry?'" I'm telling you that even the Roman guards, who are calloused to these proceedings, are listening to his words. Many can't help but lower themselves naturally in a makeshift bow to his regal nature. When others notice this obeisance, they quickly regain their arrogant attitude and exaggerate the bow as if in mockery. As I said, I have never seen anything like it. Normally I am not moved by these (almost daily) executions, primarily by crucifixion. I felt something. Not pity. Almost a release. A realization.

But I shall try to stick to the facts and not insert my own feelings, Theophilus.

Near the top of the hill, I finally caught up with Dismas. He could barely speak, and the crucifixion crew would not let me near him until they had completed their grisly work. In the meantime, I made my medical report to the clerk, who validated the execution orders and collected the stamps and paperwork for the Jewish and Roman officials. Like Jesus, Dismas dragged himself past the clerk, who then made a check mark on his list. They directed the walking dead men to their poles, where they would be roped, nailed, and hoisted upright to die over the next several days. Gesmas did not seem to be affected - defiant to the end. He sneered at the clerk.

The clerk withered under Gesmas' gaze at first then shouted, "Take this one first!" He laughed and then pointed two fingers at Dismas, checking him off the list, "You get to follow your friend." Finally, to Jesus, "I've got the best seat in the house for you, your majesty. Put him in the middle," he ordered. But the crucifixion crew ignored the clerk and grabbed Dismas first, as he was the closest, and hauled him to the upright beams and began to pinion each hand with spikes, driving the hammer without mercy. My heart skipped a beat as they missed the spike and crushed the knuckles of Dismas' left hand. As Dismas cried out, the executioners pulley-hoisted him by the cross beam up to the notch, rope tied it to the iron hook on the lateral post, and stripped his tunic from him to further humiliate him. The whole process lasted only moments, which was then repeated for Gesmas.

So they dragged Jesus, just like Dismas and Gesmas. And by now, my eyes were constantly drawn to Jesus and his words and actions rather than that of Dismas. I'm not trying to make light of the suffering of Dismas, but I am trying to report the effect Jesus had on everyone there, including me, Dismas, and Gesmas, as you shall see. I realize this goes beyond the limit of my report for Senator Graccus, Theophilus, but after you read the entire saga, you will agree that my decision was warranted.

The first hour dripped past as blood drained away from the three into the gutter, like sand from an hourglass. Gesmas seemed stepped up in a world of charcoal darkness. Seconds dribbled by, turning into painful minutes, measuring the pain by degrees, and trying to find some part of their body that did not hurt or look toward the inevitable death that would give them relief in the coming hours, or perhaps days.

The paid crowd thinned. Only true mourners and enemies remained. The soldiers settled into the boredom of waiting for hopeful cues of suffocation to emanate from the men. Another round of dice, or nine men's morris, to pass the time while listening for the coughing and gasping to mark the end of life. Once that was heard, they'd listen for gurgling exhalations as each man drowned in their own fluids. Guaging these cues, the soldiers took down another bag of wine and continued gambling, even making out-sized wagers for the meager spoils of the condemned and remaining hopeful for some action from trouble-makers and would-be rescuers.

The shrieking subsided late into the first hour. Once the cross beams had been hoisted into place and feet nailed to the toe breaks, only groanings remained. I decided this to be the best time to approach the soldiers for permission to finish my questions for Dismas. I navigated my way past the six lances, which stood ready, butt-ends in the ground, alert for action. Each lance cris-crossed the other creating an 'X' while the third remained upright, bisecting the X, tips at the ready. It reminded me of fence posts blocking sheep. The spring winds had shifted to prevail from the northwest.

Bypassing this barrier, I heard the senior Sergeant tell the youngest, "Longinus, take this robe and stretch it over the top of the spears. That wind is chilling me. Besides, maybe it'll deaden the noise from these whiners." Longinus stood, dusted the dirt from the Rabbi's tunic, and placed the robe over the top of the spears. I approached the soldiers, interrupting their games.

"I'm Doctor Luke," I reminded the soldier as he secured a cloak over the configuration of spears. "Who's in charge? I have to gather information for my report."

"You're a little too early to issue a death certificate doctor: They're still squirming. Sergeant Magnus, the one with the wine skin next to him, is the man in charge today."

I asked, "Why are you all still here, anyway? Normally, you come out, secure your prisoners, and return home to let the crows and sun finish them."

"We're here for crowd control. As I understand it, once sunset comes on, the rest of the crowd will go home for Passover. And unless Sergeant Magnus says to hurry things along, they'll hang here for days; usually three or four, or so they tell me. So you are early. Of the three, my money is on the Rabbi dying first."

"Yes. Well, I came to talk to one of the condemned," I pointed to Dismas. "I have some questions for my report."

"As I said, I'm just the new guy. Sergeant Magnus is your man. You'll want to get his permission. There's a rumor that the guy in the middle," he pointed to Jesus, "is some kind of magician - and, even worse, a politician. He's got a lot of followers in his cult. Rumor has it they may try to rescue him. But that won't happen at this point: they'd have to overwhelm us, climb the pole, pull out the nails, and figure out how to put all that blood back into his body."

Crucifixion is brutal in every way. Since the first time he was lifted up, I looked at Jesus, pinioned to the post and cross beam. Jesus was torn from head to foot, as if he had wrestled with a pride of lions. I thought he was flushed in the face until I realized blood smeared his brow, cheeks, and lips. Blood on the face tends to be a bright red because your face and head are always supplied with blood. We were well past that point. The deep purple blood of the brain and inner tissue oozed from his thorny crown. I couldn't comprehend how the wreath of thorns still stuck to his brow.

It was clear to me the thorns had not just been set upon his head and pushed into his skin from every angle holding them fast in his scalp. It was likely that even his brain was bleeding.

The rest of his body was equally abused. How was he even alive at this point? His skin, where it wasn't bleeding or bruised, was waxy white from blood loss. A large contusion appeared over his right shoulder - plainly from carrying his cross. The whipping he endured before execution produced strips of skin, which now blew in the wind like parchment. These only held fast, attached to his bones and other tendons by the thinnest flaps of tissue. The flogging had ravaged him from top to bottom and side to side.

As he exhaled, his shoulders and torso sagged with exhaustion.

He was only able to raise his chest to breathe by pushing against the toe braces.

When he pushed, the nails ripped against the holes in his feet, exacting pain while preventing a full inhalation of breath. My eyes went from the toe brace to the foot of the cross: No rain had fallen for days, yet the ground at the base of his red upright was damp and dark with the man's blood. I tried not to puke. I looked away, stifling the bile in my throat.

In trying to distract myself, I swallowed hard and tried to sound nonchalant, saying "You'd be amazed at what the body can endure," I said, pointing to the young Rabbi but looking at the soldier. "But he'll likely go today. What did he do, anyway? I see you haven't savaged the others as badly as him."

"Politics. Rome always wins. Jews, or anyone else, for that matter, always lose when going up against Rome. Tell all your friends, doctor. The other two are common murderers, thieves - nothing special. But this guy decided he wanted to rule the world, or at least this part of it. He came into Jerusalem last week to wild crowds hailing him as King. That set Herod against him. And then he stirred up the people against the Temple officials - knocking over tables, hurling insults, and, worst of all, interfering with the Temple commerce. Smart, really: get the common people on your side, then attack the institutions of order. But Pilate will not tolerate it - he's in enough trouble with Caesar. So, the Harrods, Pilates, and Temple Elders started looking for a way to catch him in the act. Between last week's parade, in which he essentially declared himself King, and that violent, riotous incitement at the Temple, enough was enough. Of course, we couldn't write all that, so we settled for King of the Jews on his titulus. The other two were easier."

He pointed to the plaque of wood above each crucified man, the Titulus, and listed his name and crime in Latin, Greek, and Aramaic. The first said, "Gesmas Ben Shakirlem, thief, murderer, liar, betrayer." The one above Dismas said, "Dismas Ben Shakirlem, thief, conspirator, accessory to murder." Above the man in the middle, its letters larger than the others, "Joshua Bar-Joseph, King of the Jews."

I thanked Longinus and approached the other five soldiers, who sat atop their cloaks in the dirt as if on a picnic. In the center, drawn in the dirt, was a game board with rocks representing each player. The man with the wine skin was rolling his dice. He threw snake eyes, cursed, and took a drink from the bag. I said, "Sergeant, I'm the physician. I want to talk with Dismas for my report, commissioned by Senator Graccus, about the Temple conspiracy. I need to know where his wife fled when you arrested him."

He looked at me with suspicion but jerked his head toward Dismas by way of permission. "Sure, Go ahead. I doubt you'll find his wife. He's only married on weekends when he has silver." All the men laughed. "Just don't get too close to the one in the middle. People who get too close to him are being watched - even his old mother. We've got them all on a list, if you know what I mean, and you don't want to be on that list."

"I won't be long. I'm not interested in him anyway. But for your information, he'll likely be dead soon. I doubt you'll have to worry about him much longer."

"Yeah, we were just talking about making it a short day if he goes quickly. We can always break the legs of the other two and hurry things along."

"I'll leave you to it, then. Thank you, Sergeant," I nodded and turned and the mayhem erupted when the next soldier threw double sixes.

~

A Mother, A Soldier, Two Thieves, And A Doctor Meet The King.

As I walked toward Dismas, passing in front of the crucified Rabbi, Jesus called out, "Father, forgive them; they know not what they do."

I stopped. "Are you talking to me, sir?" I asked, looking skyward but avoiding his gruesome countenance. He bowed his head and directed me with his eyes toward the crowd, then toward the nearby woman. His mother approached, disregarding the gawking stares of the soldiers. She looked to me, then back to the soldiers; I followed her gaze, which reached Magnus, who nodded imperceptibly. She touched my hand and looked up at her son, then at me.

"Thank you for coming. Do you know him?" she asked, taking my hand in a full but gentle grip like a mother walking her son in a busy marketplace. I thought of my mother and the last time we had held hands at she lay dying. Her hand felt familiar.

"I...I don't know him. I've heard about him, of course. Who hasn't these last few days? I'm sorry. I didn't come here to see him. I just happened to be here in the jail earlier on other business - a passer-by. But I'm sorry you have to endure this - that he has to endure such agony. His suffering won't last much longer. You should say your goodbyes. I'm saying that as a doctor. I'll be here until the end - to confirm the executioners' deaths and write my report to the authorities."

She disregarded my statement. In a calm, gentle manner - resigned to her son's fate, she said, "You can still know him. When this is all over, talk to his disciples. Come and find me. I'm Mary - his mother. I'll help you. You can write something worth reading. This," she waved her hand across the landscape, "this will all pass away soon. And he will come again. So I am telling you that he is worth knowing, even now."

Jesus called out: "I thirst..." but the soldiers ignored him and his swollen tongue, which began to protrude from his mouth. His mother turned toward the soldiers and threw a glare which was caught by Longinus, who then spoke to Magnus.

"Rantings. That one is close," Magnus said aloud to the dice thrower, "But ten drachmas says 'His Majesty' outlives them all." He took the wineskin next to him and soaked a sponge with it. "Hey, Longinus, see if His Majesty will take some wine."

Longinus put the wine-soaked sponge on the end of his spearhead. He brought it over to the foot of Jesus' cross, looking sidelong at the woman to avert her pleading glance, indeed, looking for her approval. Longinus elevated the sponge to the Rabbi's mouth and said, "If you are King of the Jews, save yourself. Bring out your army to defeat us. We are only six!" he chuckled nervously toward his fellow soldiers, who also laughed.

Longinus couldn't tell whether the Rabbi was able to pull wine from the sponge or not. He tried several times to place the sponge within reach of the man. He did not want to cause more pain. The Rabbi whispered something to Longinus and looked toward his mother with love and a nod. I couldn't make out what he said, but I could read "Longinus" on the lips of Jesus. After a few minutes, Longinus turned to Jesus' mother and me, and she nodded approval. Longinus closed his eyes in sadness and brought the now blood-soaked sponge down to remove it from the spear. He offered it to Mary, which she accepted without a word.

Returning to the group of gamblers and cleaning his spearhead, he told Sergeant Magnus, "I'll take that bet.' Looking past the Sergeant over the brow of the hill, he said, "Oh, and here comes trouble, Sergeant."

It was now well into the second hour. I was ready to make my way over to Dismas and started to let go of Mary's hand as the Temple officials arrived. They ignored the soldiers, who stood at their approach and immediately began jeering at the Rabbi, saying, "He saved others; let him save himself if he is the chosen one, the Messiah of God." Some began to pick up stones. Others spit at him. I was sure they would throw rocks at him when I saw Longinus come to the foot of his cross and shake his head as if to say: "You better be ready to deal with me. Let him die in peace."

I likewise pushed Mary behind me, interposing myself between Mary and these men. I felt like I used to when I was a shepherd protecting my sheep from a pack of wolves. Though I felt it was important to shield his mother, at the same time I believed she could hold her own against them.

"That's his mother," called one. And he lifted a rock to throw when a spear tip touched the prayer shawl at the base of his neck. "No, you don't," said Sergeant Magnus. "I'm in charge here. Unless you want to join your King, I recommend you hyenas scurry off this hill." He paused and looked west. "Looks like sunset will be here soon, and a storm's coming. Don't you have something better to do than pick on a dying man and his grieving mother?"

The chief wolf, the one with the rock, brushed aside the spear and pointed at Jesus. "You should take down that placard. It should say, 'He claimed to be the King of the Jews.'

"I wrote that - some of my best work," said Magnus. "Besides, that's what Pilate said to write. So what I have written are his words. You can take it up with him. Or, you can climb up there and change it yourself. If I were you, I'd make my way down the hill before we help you find a seat next to him. We have plenty of wood and nails, and there's always room for one more. Twelve's my record in one day."

The wolves left the hill in a bluster. Huffing and puffing their rants and derisions down the path. "Pilate will hear of this," their leader wagged, and, "This isn't over," and "Such is justice for all blasphemers." And then they blew away with the wind.

~

Today, You Will Be With Me In Paradise.

I made my way to Dismas as the storm clouds threatened. He was surprisingly alert and talkative despite his condition. Often, men in such extremes experience an infusion of vigor and alertness as the body's humors redistribute blood and serum and bile toward the head and heart and away from the extremities of hands and feet. For some, like Dismas, the result is a mistaken notion, a delirium, really, that they will somehow survive this moment. For others, an acute awareness of all that surrounds them: the mundane becomes magnified, the ignored blade of grass becomes an intricate work of art, the impending storm from which one normally would seek shelter, is anticipated for the visceral nature of the experience or drink of fresh water and rain to bathe his wounds. Time slows down into miniature moments as everything surrounding the catastrophe moves in slow motion.

As you shall see, this is what I believe was happening to Gesmas. Up to this point, I had altogether ignored Gesmas. Frankly, I didn't know him. When Dismas started his scam with Zacchaeus, Gesmas was assigned to mucking stalls on the property.

Even though they were brothers it was Gesmas who murdered the soldier. The soldiers harassed and oppressed him more than Dismas, but he remained defiant. It was clear to me that Dismas happened to be in the wrong place at the wrong time with the wrong person. Yes, Dismas was a thief and con artist, but Gesmas was a killer.

Slightly revived by the action of Longinus, Jesus began to stir. To my amazement and surprise, the Rabbi turned his head toward Gesmas and whispered something. Gesmas' responded with a guffaw and said, "What does that mean, O King? How, exactly, can you give me anything now? The only life giving water we will get is coming from those storm clouds. Then Gesmas began to revile Jesus aloud, saying, "If you are the Messiah, save yourself and us, or at least me."

Gesmas raged on, with laughter, curses, and screaming, like one possessed - or being relieved of his demons. Jesus looked at him during the tirade, taking the verbal abuse and offering no response to Gesmas.

To my amazement, timid Dismas came to the Rabbi's defense, rebuking Gesmas by saying, "Have you no fear of God, for you and I are subject to the same condemnation? And indeed, we have been condemned justly, for the sentence we received corresponds to our crimes, but this man has done nothing criminal."

Then Dismas caught the eye of the Rabbi and said, "Jesus, remember me when you come into your kingdom."

The Rabbi turned to look upon Dismas with a gaze I can only describe as pity, compassion, love. Jesus coughed and sputtered, pushing his lips apart with his swollen tongue to speak, and replied to Dismas, "Amen, I say to you, today you will be with me in Paradise."

Silence followed for some time. As the third hour approached, an eclipse of the sun covered the land in darkness. Some women and a younger man joined his mother, drawing near the foot of his cross. He spoke to them, but I could not hear what was said.

Then the Rabbi cried out in a loud voice, "Father, into Your hands I commend my spirit," and when he had said this, he breathed his last.

When the remainder of the people saw what had happened, they returned home beating their breasts; but all his family and acquaintances stood at a distance, including the women who had followed him from Galilee.

The Wager.

Dismas let out a mournful groan. Even Gesmas was softened with pity saying, "He was an innocent man." Then Gesmas looked to the crowd to spew derision on those remaining spectators, but his thirst prohibited his speaking.

"Gesmas," called Dismas across the corpse of Jesus, "We get to die today. The Rabbi told me that today I would be with Him in Paradise. Will you join us?"

"Fool!" replied Gesmas, "betting on the dying words of a tortured prophet. For what?"

"I'll take that wager," said Dismas. "I'll wager that He is Who He claimed to be - Who His enemies claimed Him to be - our King and Messiah. If I win the bet, I join Him at Abraham's bosom and stand redeemed before Yahweh. If I lose the bet, then at least I've cleansed my soul before death. I can be satisfied that I've paid my debt. Will you join me? Join us in Paradise today." Looking at the body of Jesus, he said, "He calls us."

At the death of Jesus, two witnesses testified that the soldier known as Longinus again came to the foot of Jesus' cross. He thrust his spear up into the ribs of the dead Rabbi. The witnesses reported a spray of body fluids burst from the Rabbi's corpse, splattering Longinus and misting over the crowd, offering a dew of moisture in the dark wind. Droplets drifted to the swollen lips of Gesmas, who received the blood and water as relief from his thirst, licking his lips.

"It's wine!" he called out. "Not the sour dregs offered earlier."

I could see him, in his delirium, swallowing: He swallowed, then swallowed again and again. It was as if he was pulling from a full wineskin to slake his thirst with imagined delight. No groans accompanied his phantom drinking. As a physician, I believe he was so thirsty and so pummeled with violence that he had an active dream of drinking. As I watched Gesmas finish his "drink," he seemed to ignore the nails in his wrists and feet. His eyes softened as he looked at the body of Jesus, then over to Dismas, calling out a final time to his friend, "Am I a fool? I am a fool! Relying on the dying words of a tortured prophet. But I will take your wager, Dismas. I will follow our new King to Paradise. Remember me, brother, when you enter into His Kingdom."

Longinus came to Dismas and, cudgel in hand, broke both of Dismas' legs, then did the same to Gesmas. Each man looked at the other as they struggled to breathe and looked to their newfound Messiah's dead body for hope.

Joseph, a local Sanhedrin elder, came to help Jesus' mother take down her son from the cross. I was required to certify his death as part of my official duty for the Romans. And this I did. Looking at the body, I am surprised he lasted until three o'clock. I promised Mary that I would check in on her in a few days and perhaps answer a few questions for my report. A small guard accompanied Joseph, Jesus' mother, and other women to the tomb to anoint his body and witness his internment. For some reason, the Governor had required the soldiers to seal the tomb, stand guard and report any oddities: I suppose this was a means to trap his other followers.

Not long after Jesus, the other two expired; Dismas, first, then Gesmas. After the exchange above, I did not hear either one raise enough breath to speak, at least audibly. Certifying their death was as simple as watching their lifeless bodies fall into the wagon without complaint. The only movement came from the dust that blew across their bloody remains. No family members or friends came to claim the corpses. Instead of careful descension and loving post-mortem cleansing and wrapping, the two thieves were dumped into the heap of corpses at the potter's field, with a shovel full of dry earth heaped upon them to keep the flies down. There would be no follow-up with their family, only my report.

And so, Theophilus, as I finalize my official report for Senator Graccus, leaving out some of the details above, I also send my long letter to you. Tomorrow is Sabbath, and I plan on resting! On Monday, I will check in on the dead Rabbi's mother - Mary of Nazareth, and perhaps interview her to satisfy my curiosity. I also have an appointment with a young Pharisee, Saul of Tarsus, who wanted to talk with me. These ordeals are exhausting and dirty.

As always, I appreciate our friendship and correspondence. I look forward to hearing your reaction to this narrative and will lift a toast to you until we can break bread together again.

Yours affectionately, *Luke.*

My Vision-Dream Ends.

A dust settled over my vision, Thomas, and again I saw the physician set down his pen. It seems I was peering over his shoulder now. He blew a dust over the parchment then sprinkled more powder over the drying ink. Again I saw the bodies of Dismas and Gesmas being covered with the dirt of their graves. The doctor blew on the parchment one more time, and rolled the parchment. I could feel the heat of the melted wax as he poured it over the center, affixing a seal to the edge and tying a ribbon at the center. He then slipped the writing into a hardened leather tube and secured the top.

I smelled warm bread. He dipped the end of his morsel into a pot of honey, took a bite, then picked up his stencil again and wrote: "'Man, swallow this scroll I give you, and fill yourself full.' So I ate it, and it tasted as sweet as honey."

He folded that small, separate piece of parchment into an envelope and inserted it into the pouch at the top of the tube. I was surprised I could read this writing, it being a dream and all. But I had been reading the prophet Ezekiel earlier that day. So perhaps its remnant was on my mind.

I smelled more bread and a a strong wine again. A knock sounded at my door as your brother, Jan, called to look in after me, as I've been in ill heath. He brought in a tray as I sat up. And you know, on that tray were three pieces of bread and a goblet of fine wine.

Letter to Thomas a'Kempis, Concluded.

Thomas, that is the end of my vision. I do not know if it was Heaven sent or the musings of an old man in some half-awake stupor. I must confess, I am partial to Saint Luke's account of the Gospel and have always found the story of Dismas moving and hopeful. While I am sentimental and sympathetic to Dismas, I have always wondered about Gesmas and his salvation. My dream only demonstrates that

God calls us, as he called a converted Dismas, to invite everyone to join Jesus in Paradise. As such, and given that I cannot possibly fathom God's mercy, I am hopeful that those who meet Jesus, who accept His claims, who follow Him up Calvary's Hill, even if they challenge His Kingship, will still be offered a place in paradise with Him in those last moments.

But they must accept Him. God will not force Himself upon us. In the end, I believe Gesmas, like his brother, wagered correctly. Gesmas was fortunate to have a brother like Dismas. Dismas was fortunate to recognize Jesus and His Kingship. God will accept a weak wager from a weak man; our two-pennies worth, for we are worth even more than many sparrows!

As a priest of God, you will be Christ to others. Literally acting *in persona Christi*. As you imitate Christ, as a priest, consecrating and feeding those who follow Christ; as you consume His Body and Blood, you are imitating Christ feeding five thousand, ten thousand, more! How many thousands during a lifetime?

As you do so, you are encountering the cynical, deeply stained Dismases of the world and inviting them to meet you in paradise. And yes, you will meet plenty of Gesmases. You will pray for them, invite them, feed them, serve them. On this side of Heaven, you will always wonder if you will meet in Paradise. But God does not wonder. His Mercy is infinite. He Thirsts for their souls, and so will you. Some days you will be Jesus to them. Some days Dismas. Some days, Luke. Some days, Mary. As a priest you can offer bread of the finest wheat and wine of the choicest grapes. Often they will only see the elements, scoff at the bread, criticize the wine. But they will still hunger and thirst until He reveals Himself to them in the breaking of the bread. He will use you, Thomas, to reveal Himself to many.

Yours in Christ,
Prior Radewyns

THE INSTALLATION OF ADRIAAN BOEYENS

Editor's Note: What happened to Adriaan Boeyens? Enjoy this short story to find out!

~

The wood lathe covered wagon ambled up to the Vatican's city gates. It could've easily been mistaken for a street peddler's wagon or even that of an itinerant entertainer - with room enough for sleeping and trade tools. The guard stepped out from under the umbrella pine's shade into the blazing sun as the wagon wheel dust collided with his uniform trousers, covering the napkin that lay atop the face of his sleeping partner.

The guard raised his bandanna so he wouldn't breathe in the fine road dust. Then batted the dust from his uniform, wiped his brow and called out: "Papers? State your business. I am Tomaso, guard to the Vatican."

Pedro, the driver, not understanding the dialect, replied "No entiendo. No hablo italiano." Pedro turned round, opened the curtains to the wagon bed and whispered in Spanish, "Lord, the guard wants to know our business, and I don't speak the language. Please, can you speak with him?" Pedro's horse snorted, dropping a pile of dung.

As if on cue, a priest, wearing a common monk's robe, pushed through the curtains, and addressed the guard. "I am Father Adrian Boeyens, here on official business of the Vatican. I was told that we are expected."

The guard looked down at his board, running his finger along the list of names. "I'm sorry Father, can you show me your name? And anyway, I can't read, as that is Guido's job, and, as you can see he is indisposed. If you can show me your papers with your name, I can compare the two. That will be good enough for me, although I will still need you to write down the nature of your business next to your name. And please, have your driver clean up after his horse here. We can't have the new Holy Father come through a gate strewn with horse dung! We've been waiting for Him since January. We thought maybe he was setting up shop in Spain."

Father Adrian ignored the comment as he poured over the list of names and, not seeing his own, produced the scroll stamped with the Spanish Emperor's seal. "My name is not here, I'll look again, but in the mean time, these are my papers. I am here for the Papal installation. I can write that out for you or you can wake Guido to verify my permission to enter the city."

"I apologize for the delay, Father, we have very strict orders, especially from Vatican City. One of these days we expect the new Pope. But these Popes, you know, with respect, they come into the city with parades and tributes and salutes. It's chaos. And everyone wants to be here. And everyone thinks they are special. Do you know how many priests we get here who expect to be on the Vatican's list?

"Hi Holiness Leo, the last one, rest his soul, was a big spender - a Medici, you know. His party went on for some time; some say eight years. And while he didn't exactly sell tickets, I heard you could get out of Purgatory for contributing to his installation...or maybe it was Hell - I think it depended on the amount of coinage and the type of sin. Leo, apparently, allowed prepayment for sins not yet committed. Such a deal. Anyway, that was eight years ago. I was still a guard-apprentice, but had a good time: these foreigners think you are somebody when you wear a uniform and guard a gate. Or they think you are part of the Swiss guard started by Julius. I do like their uniforms, I must say. But yes, this fine uniform is how I met my wife, also a foreigner - a Florentine, part of the Medici entourage. She says she's the bastard child of one of the Medici. But so is half the city. She still works at the Vatican, taking in the washing from the cardinal arch-bishop there - she say he's her brother. I don't know. But I got promoted to full guard not long after he took the red hat. Anything helps pay the cost of living in this town. We can barely afford to pay attention, let alone buy our way to Heaven. Old Leo X, had taxes on his taxes. They say he liked taxing people ten times over, in recognition of being Leo the tenth! I don't know. But supposedly the till is somehow empty. When the malaria came and killed him, they said it was because the doctor demanded payment up front and Leo couldn't pay the doctor. I don't know. The next morning he woke up, he was dead!

"So we needed a new pope. They tell me no one wanted the job! Even though everyone wants the job. No one wants to face the music of the debt. The creditors have been lining up ever since Leo's funeral. They are even selling his elephant!

"My wife tells me that no one wanted this Dutch priest to be the pope, but they couldn't agree on who to pick, and since he wasn't here, and no one really liked him - or more to the point, everyone liked that he wasn't a Medici or a Borja, the elected him. The Florentines hated the Spanish, who hated the English, who wanted Cardinal Woolsey. I've met Woolsey, you know. They couldn't agree on Cardinal Woolsey or that Medici bastard, Guilio - the dead Pope's cousin. All they could agree on was this Dutchman. So the elected him: up went the white smoke. 'Poof poof poof.' Even the smoke had to be coerced up the chimney because of the downdraft. A bad omen for this one.

"And can you imagine? Not being here for the papal election and finding out by letter that you are the new Pope! It must've seemed a bad joke to him. It's certainly taken long enough for his response: it's been eight months and still no 'Habemus Papa!' No parades, no parties. Every day the papal footman comes out on the porch and sweeps it, just in case. The only change around here these last months has been winter turning to spring and spring to summer. You see, even the flies are hungry for change. Perhaps the new pope will take the elephant and offer these flies a change of diet."

Flies gathered at the fresh horse droppings, hoping for a respite from the dry heat. "Not only do we not have a pope, but God sent us this blast furnace of a summer. I tell you it's a sign: there's been no rain in over a month. The wells are drying up. Cisterns are low, fountains are empty. If we don't get rain soon, the vineyard grapes will turn to raisins. The flies bite relentlessly in protest, looking for a drink of sweat. Look at them feast on the dung!"

Tomaso took back the list from the priest and continued, "Usually we have lists of all His Holiness's emissaries. I am sorry you didn't make the list, but appreciate that you are not angry. Are you angry?"

Father Adrian waited with patient attention and a wry smile. Guido stirred under the napkin, swatting a fly. "No, my son. I am not surprised I did not make the list. I fear it may be a while before I rate that highly in this city, if I ever do."

"Yes, Father, every day Guido asks for a list of the new Pope's clerks and servants. I look forward to the busy days of inspecting the food wagons for the installation celebration. I usually get good samples! It should be a great feast; although I've heard this new pope is a bit tight-fisted. A Dutch Pope - do you expect less from a Dutchman Father?

"Well, whenever he comes, we'll be logging visitors by the hundreds every day and those thieving Red Hats will want an accounting so His Holiness can repay them for all the party favors that come through that gate. After that, there will be grand parades and trumpets and flags and so forth. And more taxes, more indulgences, more poverty. So can you please tell me the nature of your business and write it here for me in my ledger? Guido usually does that, but as you can see, he's busy checking that napkin for holes. I don't want to disturb him."

"Yes. We will see. Give me your log book," commanded the priest. Adrian sat in the vacant teamster's chair and wrote. Pedro collected the dung and looked at Tomaso for direction. Tomaso pointed to Guido's sleeping body, and motioned Pedro, with a laugh, to put the pile of horse dung under the sleeping guard's cot. The hungry flies followed.

"I found it!" The priest passed the sheaf of parchments back to the Tomaso. "Here, Tomaso, I circled my name on your sheet. May I call on you from time to time? I need men who know what is happening in this city. Perhaps I can send your wife my laundry as well, if your wife does as good a job as you say."

"Thank you, Father. I will gladly take you up on your offer. Be careful as you enter this den of thieves. They act like sheep, but there are several wolves among them - you'll know them by their red hats. Now, Pedro, just aim your nag toward the bell tower on your left. You can't miss the stables."

Father Adrian translated, then went behind the curtain to settled back under the covered wagon, Pedro clucked his tongue and the horse moved off.

A voice groaned from the under shade tree, "What is with these flies?"

"Just a little fun," laughed Tomaso. "Giving a visitor some directions. Here, he finally found his name on the list."

Tomaso passed the parchment to Guido, pointing out the circled name. The blood drained from Guido's face. His eyes widened. "Are you sure this is the man? What did he say?"

"Father Adrian. From Spain. Funny, he didn't have a Spanish accent. More German, but his Italian was perfect, though he dropped in some Latin here and there. Why? What's the big deal? Should I have had him underline instead of circle?"

"No, you idiot. That...that was no 'Father Adrian.' That was Cardinal Adrian Florens Dedal Boyens of Utrech."

"So? He just said Father Adrian to me."

"That man, that man is the new Pope!"

<<END>>

PART III: LORD OF THE WORLD
A PROLOGUE BY MONSIGNOR ROBERT HUGH BENSON

The following prologue is from the novel by Monsignor Robert Hugh Benson.

Monsignor Benson wrote the book, The Lord of the World, to wide acclaim when it was published in 1907. It was seen as a work to be reckoned with as new technologies, alliances and organizations arose with a background of rising nationalism.

The full novel, with a brief biography of Monsignor Benson and other commentary, will be punished in early 2024 by Timothy E. Moore. Look for it at your favorite Catholic bookstore, at my website (timothyedmoore.com) on at online bookstores.

LORD OF THE WORLD: PROLOGUE

Persons who do not like tiresome prologues, need not read this one. It is essential only to the situation, not to the story.
-RHB

"You must give me a moment," said the old man, leaning back.

PERCY RESETTLED himself in his chair and waited, chin on hand.

IT WAS A VERY silent room in which the three men sat, furnished with the extreme common sense of the period. It had neither window nor door; for it was now sixty years since the world, recognizing that space is not confined to the surface of the globe, had begun to burrow in earnest. Old Mr. Templeton's house stood some forty feet below the level of the Thames embankment, in what was considered a somewhat commodious position, for he had only a hundred yards to walk before he reached the station of the Second Central Motor-circle, and a quarter of a mile to the volor-station at Blackfriars. He was over ninety years old, however, and seldom left his house now. The room itself was lined throughout with the delicate green jade-enamel prescribed by the Board of Health, and was suffused with the artificial sunlight discovered by the great Reuter forty years before; it had the colour-tone of a spring wood, and was warmed and venti-lated through the classical frieze grating to the exact

temperature of 18 degrees Centigrade. Mr. Templeton was a plain man, content to live as his father had lived before him. The furniture, too, was a little old-fashioned in make and design, constructed however according to the prevailing system of soft asbestos enamel welded over iron, indestructible, pleasant to the touch, and resem-bling mahogany. A couple of book-cases well filled ran on either side of the bronze pedestal electric fire before which sat the three men; and in the further corners stood the hydraulic lifts that gave entrance, the one to the bedroom, the other to the corridor fifty feet up which opened on to the Embankment.

Father Percy Franklin, the elder of the two priests, was rather a remarkable-looking man, not more than thirty-five years old, but with hair that was white throughout; his grey eyes, under black eyebrows, were peculiarly bright and almost passionate; but his prominent nose and chin and the extreme decisiveness of his mouth reassured the observer as to his will. Strangers usually looked twice at him.

Father Francis, however, sitting in his upright chair on the other side of the hearth, brought down the average; for, though his brown eyes were pleasant and pathetic, there was no strength in his face; there was even a tendency to feminine melancholy in the corners of his mouth and the marked droop of his eyelids.

Mr. Templeton was just a very old man, with a strong face in folds, clean-shaven like the rest of the world, and was now lying back on his water-pillows with the quilt over his feet.

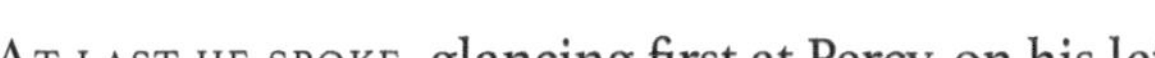

AT LAST HE SPOKE, glancing first at Percy, on his left.

"Well," he said, "it is a great business to remember exactly; but this is how I put it to myself."

"In England our party was first seriously alarmed at the Labour Parliament of 1917. That showed us how deeply Herveism had impregnated the whole social atmosphere. There had been Socialists before, but none like Gustave Herve in his old age--at least no one of the same power. He, perhaps you have read, taught absolute Materialism and Socialism developed to their logical issues. Patriotism, he said, was a relic of barbarism; and sensual enjoyment was the only certain good. Of course, every one laughed at him. It was said that without religion there could be no adequate motive among the masses for even the simplest social order. But he was right, it seemed. After the fall of the French Church at the beginning of the century and the massacres of 1914, the bourgeoisie settled down to organise itself; and that extraordinary movement began in earnest, pushed through by the middle classes, with no patriotism, no class distinctions, practically no army. Of course, Freemasonry directed it all. This spread to Germany, where the influence of Karl Marx had already---"

"Yes, sir," put in Percy smoothly, "but what of England, if you don't mind---"

"Ah, yes; England. Well, in 1917 the Labour party gathered up the reins, and Communism really began. That was long before I can remember, of course, but my father used to date it from then. The only wonder was that things did not go forward more quickly; but I suppose there was a good deal of Tory leaven left. Besides, centuries generally run slower than is expected, especially after beginning with an impulse. But the new order began then; and the Communists have never suffered a serious reverse since, except the little one in '25. Blenkin founded 'The New People' then; and the 'Times' dropped out; but it was not, strangely enough, till '35 that the House of Lords fell for the last time. The Established Church had gone finally in '29."

"And the religious effect of that?" asked Percy swiftly, as the old man paused to cough slightly, lifting his inhaler. The priest was anxious to keep to the point.

"It was an effect itself," said the other, "rather than a cause. You see, the Ritualists, as they used to call them, after a desperate attempt to get into the Labour swim, came into the Church after the Convocation of '19, when the Nicene Creed dropped out; and there was no real enthusiasm except among them. But so far as there was an effect from the final Disestablishment, I think it was that what was left of the State Church melted into the Free Church, and the Free Church was, after all, nothing more than a little sentiment. The Bible was completely given up as an authority after the renewed German attacks in the twenties; and the Divinity of our Lord, some think, had gone all but in name by the beginning of the century. The Kenotic theory had provided for that. Then there was that strange little movement among the Free Churchmen even earlier; when ministers who did no more than follow the swim--who were sensitive to draughts, so to speak--broke off from their old positions. It is curious to read in the history of the time how they were hailed as independent thinkers. It was just exactly what they were not.... Where was I? Oh, yes.... Well, that cleared the ground for us, and the Church made extraordinary progress for a while--extraordinary, that is, under the circumstances, because you must remember, things were very different from twenty, or even ten, years before. I mean that, roughly speaking, the severing of the sheep and the goats had begun. The religious people were practically all Catholics and Individualists; the irreligious people rejected the supernatural altogether, and were, to a man, Materialists and Communists. But we made progress because we had a few exceptional men--Delaney the philosopher, McArthur and Largent, the philanthropists, and so on. It really seemed as if Delaney and his disciples might carry everything before them. You remember his 'Analogy'? Oh, yes, it is all in the text-books....

"Well, then, at the close of the Vatican Council, which had been called in the nineteenth century, and never dissolved, we lost a great number through the final definitions. The 'Exodus of the Intellectuals' the world called it---"

"The Biblical decisions," put in the younger priest.

"That partly; and the whole conflict that began with the rise of Modernism at the beginning of the century but much more the condemnation of Delaney, and of the New Transcendentalism generally, as it was then understood. He died outside the Church, you know. Then there was the condemnation of Sciotti's book on Comparative Religion.... After that the Communists went on by strides, although by very slow ones. It seems extraordinary to you, I dare say, but you cannot imagine the excitement when the Necessary Trades Bill became law in '60. People thought that all enterprise would stop when so many professions were nationalised; but, you know, it didn't. Certainly the nation was behind it."

"What year was the Two-Thirds Majority Bill passed?" asked Percy.

"Oh! long before--within a year or two of the fall of the House of Lords. It was necessary, I think, or the Individualists would have gone raving mad.... Well, the Necessary Trades Bill was inevitable: people had begun to see that even so far back as the time when the railways were municipalised. For a while there was a burst of art; because all the Individualists who could went in for it (it was then that the Toller school was founded); but they soon drifted back into Government employment; after all, the six-per-cent limit for all individual enterprise was not much of a temptation; and Government paid well."

Percy shook his head.

"Yes; but I cannot understand the present state of affairs. You said just now that things went slowly?"

"Yes," said the old man, "but you must remember the Poor Laws. That established the Communists for ever. Certainly Braithwaite knew his business."

The younger priest looked up inquiringly.

"The abolition of the old workhouse system," said Mr. Templeton. "It is all ancient history to you, of course; but I remember as if it was yesterday. It was that which brought down what was still called the Monarchy and the Universities."

"Ah," said Percy. "I should like to hear you talk about that, sir."

"Presently, father.... Well, this is what Braithwaite did. By the old system all paupers were treated alike, and resented it. By the new system there were the three grades that we have now, and the enfranchisement of the two higher grades. Only the absolutely worthless were assigned to the third grade, and treated more or less as criminals--of course after careful examination. Then there was the reorganisation of the Old Age Pensions. Well, don't you see how strong that made the Communists? The Individualists--they were still called Tories when I was a boy--the Individualists have had no chance since. They are no more than a worn-out drag now. The whole of the working classes--and that meant ninety-nine of a hundred--were all against them."

Percy looked up; but the other went on.

"Then there was the Prison Reform Bill under Macpherson, and the abolition of capital punishment; there was the final Education Act of '59, whereby dogmatic secularism was established; the practical abolition of inheritance under the reformation of the Death Duties---"

"I forget what the old system was," said Percy.

"Why, it seems incredible, but the old system was that all paid alike. First came the Heirloom Act, and then the change by which inherited wealth paid three times the duty of earned wealth, leading up to the acceptance of Karl Marx's doctrines in '89--but the former came in '77.... Well, all these things kept England up to the level of the Continent; she had only been just in time to join in with the final scheme of Western Free Trade. That was the first effect, you remember, of the Socialists' victory in Germany."

"And how did we keep out of the Eastern War?" asked Percy anxiously.

"Oh! that's a long story; but, in a word, America stopped us; so we lost India and Australia. I think that was the nearest to the downfall of the Communists since '25. But Braithwaite got out of it very cleverly by getting us the protectorate of South Africa once and for all. He was an old man then, too."

Mr. Templeton stopped to cough again. Father Francis sighed and shifted in his chair.

"And America?" asked Percy.

"Ah! all that is very complicated. But she knew her strength and annexed Canada the same year. That was when we were at our weakest."

Percy stood up.

"Have you a Comparative Atlas, sir?" he asked.

The old man pointed to a shelf.

"There," he said.

PERCY LOOKED at the sheets a minute or two in silence, spreading them on his knees.

"It is all much simpler, certainly," he murmured, glancing first at the old complicated colouring of the beginning of the twentieth century, and then at the three great washes of the twenty-first.

He moved his finger along Asia. The words EASTERN EMPIRE ran across the pale yellow, from the Ural Mountains on the left to the Behring Straits on the right, curling round in giant letters through India, Australia, and New Zealand. He glanced at the red; it was considerably smaller, but still important enough, considering that it covered not only Europe proper, but all Russia up to the Ural Mountains, and Africa to the south. The blue-labelled AMERICAN REPUBLIC swept over the whole of that continent, and disappeared right round to the left of the Western Hemisphere in a shower of blue sparks on the white sea.

"Yes, it's simpler," said the old man drily.

Percy shut the book and set it by his chair.

"And what next, sir? What will happen?"

The old Tory statesman smiled.

"God knows," he said. "If the Eastern Empire chooses to move, we can do nothing. I don't know why they have not moved. I suppose it is because of religious differences."

"Europe will not split?" asked the priest.

"No, no. We know our danger now. And America would certainly help us. But, all the same, God help us--or you, I should rather say--if the Empire does move! She knows her strength at last."

There was silence for a moment or two. A faint vibration trembled through the deep-sunk room as some huge machine went past on the broad boulevard overhead.

"Prophesy, sir," said Percy suddenly. "I mean about religion."

Mr. Templeton inhaled another long breath from his instrument. Then again he took up his discourse.

"Briefly," he said, "there are three forces--Catholicism, Humanitarianism, and the Eastern religions. About the third I cannot prophesy, though I think the Sufis will be victorious. Anything may happen; Esotericism is making enormous strides--and that means Pantheism; and the blending of the Chinese and Japanese dynasties throws out all our calculations. But in Europe and America, there is no doubt that the struggle lies between the other two. We can neglect everything else. And, I think, if you wish me to say what I think, that, humanly speaking, Catholicism will decrease rapidly now. It is perfectly true that Protestantism is dead. Men do recognise at last that a supernatural Religion involves an absolute authority, and that Private Judgment in matters of faith is nothing else than the beginning of disintegration. And it is also true that since the Catholic Church is the only institution that even claims supernatural authority, with all its merciless logic, she has again the allegiance of practically all Christians who have any supernatural belief left. There are a few faddists left, especially in America and here; but they are negligible. That is all very well; but, on the other hand, you must remember that Humanitarianism, contrary to all persons' expectations, is becoming an actual religion itself, though anti-supernatural. It is Pantheism; it is developing a ritual under Freemasonry; it has a creed, 'God is Man,' and the rest. It has therefore a real food of a sort to offer to religious cravings; it idealises, and yet it makes no demand upon the spiritual faculties. Then, they have the use of all the churches except ours, and all the Cathedrals; and they are beginning at last to encourage sentiment. Then, they may display their symbols and we may not: I think that they will be established legally in another ten years at the latest.

"Now, we Catholics, remember, are losing; we have lost steadily for more than fifty years. I suppose that we have, nominally, about one-fortieth of America now--and that is the result of the Catholic movement of the early twenties. In France and Spain we are nowhere; in Germany we are less. We hold our position in the East, certainly; but even there we have not more than one in two hundred-- so the statistics say--and we are scattered. In Italy? Well, we have Rome again to ourselves, but nothing else; here, we have Ireland altogether and perhaps one in sixty of England, Wales and Scotland; but we had one in forty seventy years ago. Then there is the enormous progress of psychology--all clean against us for at least a century. First, you see, there was Materialism, pure and simple that failed more or less--it was too crude--until psychology came to the rescue. Now psychology claims all the rest of the ground; and the supernatural sense seems accounted for. That's the claim. No, father, we are losing; and we shall go on losing, and I think we must even be ready for a catastrophe at any moment."

"But---" began Percy.

"You think that weak for an old man on the edge of the grave. Well, it is what I think. I see no hope. In fact, it seems to me that even now something may come on us quickly. No; I see no hope until---"

Percy looked up sharply.

"Until our Lord comes back," said the old statesman.

Father Francis sighed once more, and there fell a silence.

"And the fall of the Universities?" said Percy at last.

"My dear father, it was exactly like the fall of the Monasteries under Henry VIII--the same results, the same arguments, the same incidents. They were the strongholds of Individualism, as the Monasteries were the strongholds of Papalism; and they were regarded with the same kind of awe and envy. Then the usual sort of remarks began about the amount of port wine drunk; and suddenly people said that they had done their work, that the inmates were mistaking means for ends; and there was a great deal more reason for saying it. After all, granted the supernatural, Religious Houses are an obvious consequence; but the object of secular education is presumably the production of something visible--either character or competence; and it became quite impossible to prove that the Universities produced either--which was worth having. The distinction between ου and με[Greek words for you and me.

Ou =

Με =] is not an end in itself; and the kind of person produced by its study was not one which appealed to England in the twentieth century. I am not sure that it appealed even to me much (and I was always a strong Individualist)--except by way of pathos---"

"Yes?" said Percy.

"Oh, it was pathetic enough. The Science Schools of Cambridge and the Colonial Department of Oxford were the last hope; and then those went. The old dons crept about with their books, but nobody wanted them--they were too purely theoretical; some drifted into the poorhouses, first or second grade; some were taken care of by charitable clergymen; there was that attempt to concentrate in Dublin; but it failed, and people soon forgot them. The buildings, as you know, were used for all kinds of things. Oxford became an engineering establishment for a while, and Cambridge a kind of Government laboratory. I was at King's College, you know. Of course it was all as horrible as it could be--though I am glad they kept the chapel open even as a museum. It was not nice to see the chantries filled with anatomical specimens. However, I don't think it was much worse than keeping stoves and surplices in them."

"What happened to you?"

"Oh! I was in Parliament very soon; and I had a little money of my own, too. But it was very hard on some of them; they had little pensions, at least all who were past work. And yet, I don't know: I suppose it had to come. They were very little more than picturesque survivals, you know; and had not even the grace of a religious faith about them."

Percy sighed again, looking at the humorously reminiscent face of the old man. Then he suddenly changed the subject again.

"What about this European parliament?" he said.

The old man started.

"Oh!... I think it will pass," he said, "if a man can be found to push it. All this last century has been leading up to it, as you see. Patriotism has been dying fast; but it ought to have died, like slavery and so forth, under the influence of the Catholic Church. As it is, the work has been done without the Church; and the result is that the world is beginning to range itself against us: it is an organised antagonism -- a kind of Catholic anti-Church. Democracy has done what the Divine Monarchy should have done. If the proposal passes I think we may expect something like persecution once more.... But, again, the Eastern invasion may save us, if it comes off.... I do not know...."

Percy sat still yet a moment; then he stood up suddenly.

"I must go, sir," he said, relapsing into Esperanto. "It is past nineteen o'clock. Thank you so much. Are you coming, father?"

Father Francis stood up also, in the dark grey suit permitted to priests, and took up his hat.

"Well, father," said the old man again, "come again some day, if I haven't been too discursive. I suppose you have to write your letter yet?"

Percy nodded.

"I did half of it this morning," he said, "but I felt I wanted another bird's-eye view before I could understand properly: I am so grateful to you for giving it me. It is really a great labour, this daily letter to the Cardinal-Protector. I am thinking of resigning if I am allowed."

"My dear father, don't do that. If I may say so to your face, I think you have a very shrewd mind; and unless Rome has balanced information she can do nothing. I don't suppose your colleagues are as careful as yourself."

Percy smiled, lifting his dark eyebrows deprecatingly.

"Come, father," he said.

❧

THE TWO PRIESTS parted at the steps of the corridor, and Percy stood for a minute or two staring out at the familiar autumn scene, trying to understand what it all meant. What he had heard downstairs seemed strangely to illuminate that vision of splendid prosperity that lay before him.

The air was as bright as day; artificial sunlight had carried all before it, and London now knew no difference between dark and light. He stood in a kind of glazed cloister, heavily floored with a preparation of rubber on which footsteps made no sound. Beneath him, at the foot of the stairs, poured an endless double line of persons severed by a partition, going to right and left, noiselessly, except for the murmur of Esperanto talking that sounded ceaselessly as they went. Through the clear, hardened glass of the public passage showed a broad sleek black roadway, ribbed from side to side, and puckered in the centre, significantly empty, but even as he stood there a note sounded far away from Old Westminster, like the hum of a giant hive, rising as it came, and an instant later a transparent thing shot past, flashing from every angle, and the note died to a hum again and a silence as the great Government motor from the south whirled eastwards with the mails. This was a privileged roadway; nothing but state-vehicles were allowed to use it, and those at a speed not exceeding one hundred miles an hour.

Other noises were subdued in this city of rubber; the passenger-circles were a hundred yards away, and the subterranean traffic lay too deep for anything but a vibration to make itself felt. It was to remove this vibration, and silence the hum of the ordinary vehicles, that the Government experts had been working for the last twenty years.

Once again before he moved there came a long cry from over-head, startlingly beautiful and piercing, and, as he lifted his eyes from the glimpse of the steady river which alone had refused to be trans-formed, he saw high above him against the heavy illuminated clouds, a long slender object, glowing with soft light, slide northwards and vanish on outstretched wings. That musical cry, he told himself, was the voice of one of the European line of volors announcing its arrival in the capital of Great Britain.

"Until our Lord comes back," he thought to himself; and for an instant the old misery stabbed at his heart. How difficult it was to hold the eyes focussed on that far horizon when this world lay in the foreground so compelling in its splendour and its strength! Oh, he had argued with Father Francis an hour ago that size was not the same as greatness, and that an insistent external could not exclude a subtle internal; and he had believed what he had then said; but the doubt yet remained till he silenced it by a fierce effort, crying in his heart to the Poor Man of Nazareth to keep his heart as the heart of a little child.

Then he set his lips, wondering how long Father Francis would bear the pressure, and went down the steps.

Look for the Full Publication in late 2024 on my website: timothyedmoore.com

*As always, I dedicate my writing to my lovely wife, Donna, and our amazing children and their children:
Cordelia and Antti, Virginia and Adam, Jim and Elissa, Joe and Haylee, Josh, Maria, and John Paul. I pray for you and your children (present and future) daily.
I also want to dedicate this book to the memory of my friend, Kevin Vost, who is enjoying the Beatific Vision. He went to Heaven shortly after Easter of this year (2023). He has been, and still is, a mentor and inspiration to me. Kevin, please pray for us.
Tim Moore, Feast of Corpus Christi, 2023.*

ABOUT THE AUTHOR

Timothy E. "Tim" Moore lives and writes in Springfield, Illinois.

Tim has spent the last decade writing about *The Imitation of Christ*, which has led him on many a journey, including a pilgrimage to the Zwolle, NL, where Thomas' remains are housed in the Church of the Assumption of Mary. See Tim's post below for more details https://www.timothyedmoore.com/why-isnt-thomas-akempis-a-saint-of-the-catholic-church/

Tim has now written commentaries and fictional narratives on all four books of *The Imitation of Christ*. You can find these on his website: timothyedmoore.com, at good Catholic bookstores, and on many online bookstores.

These books will soon be available in audio format as well. Check his website for updates.

For a free e-copy of Tim's short story about St. Nicholas, *Nicholas the Peddler*, email your request to: Tim@timothyedmoore.com.

Tim continues to edit other great but lesser known books, like *Lord of the World*, by Monsignor Robert Hugh Benson, as well as his own short stories and novels and devotionals.

ALSO BY THOMAS A'KEMPIS
AND TIMOTHY E. MOORE

The Imitation of Christ Book 1

The Imitation of Christ Book 2

The Imitation of Christ Book 3

www.ingramcontent.com/pod-product-compliance
Lightning Source LLC
Chambersburg PA
CBHW030314160726
47992CB00005B/2006